TABBY IN THE TUB

Mrs. Ward's face looked troubled. "So what does this mean for Delilah's kittens?"

"One option is to find a cat who has lost her own kittens, to act as a foster mother until Delilah is fully recovered." Dr. Emily paused. "Unfortunately I don't know of any such cats at the moment, and even if I did there's no guarantee that she would accept the kittens anyway."

"Is there another option?" asked Bill Ward.

Dr. Emily sighed. "Bearing in mind you both work, hand-rearing would be virtually impossible. The other option is to put them to sleep."

Mandy gasped, horrified.

Not trusting herself to speak, she turned and ran into the residential unit, collapsing in a heap by the door. Surely the Wards wouldn't put Delilah's kittens to sleep? How could they? If only there was something she could do. She thought of how the kittens had been earlier that day, play-fighting and toddling around their box. But it was the Wards' decision. Burying her head in her hands, she cried noisily.

Give someone you love a home!
Read about the animals of Animal Ark™

TABBY
in the TUB

Ben M. Baglio

Illustrations by Jenny Gregory

Cover illustration by
Mary Ann Lasher

AN
APPLE
PAPERBACK

SCHOLASTIC INC.
New York Toronto London Auckland Sydney
Mexico City New Delhi Hong Kong Buenos Aires

**Special thanks to Linda Chapman.
Thanks also to C. J. Hall, B. Vet. Med., M.R.C.V.S., for reviewing
the veterinary information contained in this book.**

ISBN 0-439-34390-9

12 11   3 4 5 6 7/0

Printed in the U.S.A.   40
First Scholastic printing, February 2002

One

Mandy Hope and James Hunter cycled out of Welford village. Daffodils nodded in the spring sunshine as they passed. "I've got a biology test today," Mandy groaned. "I looked over it for two hours last night and I still haven't learned it."

Mandy knew that if she wanted to be a vet then she had to do well in school, but she hated studying for tests. There were always so many other things that she would rather be doing — like looking after the animals that came into Animal Ark, her parents' veterinary practice.

"You'll do fine," James, her best friend, reassured her. They approached the last row of houses. "Race you up

1

the hill!" he called. Not waiting for Mandy's answer, he put his head down, his brown hair flopping over his face, and started to pedal like mad.

"That's not fair!" Mandy protested, pedaling furiously after him.

As James sped past the first house, Mandy's sharp eyes noticed a cat coming out of one of the cottage gates just ahead of him. It was a white Persian cat. A very pregnant, white Persian cat who was heading straight toward the road.

James's eyes were looking down as he tried to make the most of his head start.

"James!" Mandy yelled. "Look out!"

The cat stepped out, her head held high. Her large, cumbersome body swayed as she walked.

"Stop!" cried Mandy in horror.

At the very last moment, James saw the cat. He jammed on his brakes and his bike skewed violently to one side, missing the cat by inches.

James and the bike crashed to the ground.

Mandy screeched to a halt and flung her bike onto the pavement. She raced over to the cat and scooped her up. Was she all right? Were there any signs of shock? The cat's rough tongue flicked over Mandy's hand and she rubbed her head against Mandy's chin. She wasn't

hurt, just rather surprised at having such an unexpected cuddle. "Oh, thank goodness!" Mandy whispered, hugging her close.

Suddenly she remembered James and looked across the road.

He was gingerly disentangling himself from his bike. "Are you all right?" Mandy asked, hurrying over.

"I think so," said James, pushing his glasses firmly back onto his nose. He looked anxiously at the cat in Mandy's arms. "How is she?"

"Okay, I think," Mandy said, stroking the cat's soft white fur. "It's Delilah. You know — she belongs to Mr. Ward."

James nodded and stroked the cat's head. Bill Ward was the village mailman. They often passed him doing his rounds on their way to school. "He brought her in to Animal Ark a couple of weeks ago for a checkup on her pregnancy," Mandy said. Delilah looked up at her and purred.

"When are her kittens due?" James asked, wheeling his bike off the road.

"In about two weeks, I think," said Mandy. She looked around at the row of pretty gray-stone cottages that nestled together, with sloping roofs and tiny windows. "We can't leave her out here. Shall we see if Mrs. Ward is in?"

"Which house is it?" James asked.

Mandy nodded toward a cottage near the end of the row. "The one with the pink cherry tree in the yard."

Each of the cottages had a front yard bordered by a shrubbery hedge. James pushed open the wooden gate that led into the Wards' yard. The spring breeze sent fluffy pieces of pale-pink cherry blossoms swirling around Mandy's head. Two terra-cotta pots stood by the front door, purple and white pansies spilling out of them. James reached the door and knocked loudly. A dog barked inside and they heard footsteps approaching.

"Back, Tara!" said a voice inside, and Jane Ward, the mailman's wife, opened the door. She was dressed in jeans and a sweatshirt. A black-and-tan dog, about the size of a small Labrador, attempted to wriggle past her but she caught its collar quickly. "Steady, Tara." As she caught sight of Delilah in Mandy's arms, her inquiring look changed to one of surprise. "Delilah! How did you get outside?"

"We found her crossing the road," Mandy explained.

"I almost ran her over," admitted James, rather shamefaced.

"But we think she's all right," said Mandy quickly, seeing a look of concern cross Mrs. Ward's face. "James didn't touch her."

"I must have forgotten to lock the cat-door flap," groaned Jane, running a hand through her curly blond hair. "Thank you so much for bringing her back in. I've been trying to keep her in the house, unless I'm outside to keep an eye on her. Her road sense has been terrible since she got pregnant."

Tara, the dog, was still struggling to greet Mandy and James. Giving up the battle, Jane released her hold on the collar and Tara bounded out joyfully.

James grabbed her just in time to stop her from jumping up at Mandy and Delilah. "Whoa, Tara!" The dog licked his face and hands ecstatically. She was an Australian cattle dog, square-shaped, strong and sturdy, with a head a bit like a German shepherd's. James and Mandy had first met Tara when she was just a few months old, and the Wards had bought her to keep Delilah company. Her heavy tail thwacked against James's legs. "She's as lively as always!" said James with a grin.

Jane smiled and took Delilah from Mandy. "It's certainly quite a job keeping an eye on both of them." She put Delilah down and sighed as the cat stalked slowly toward the kitchen. "I don't know what I'm going to do with Delilah. She's never been good with traffic, but she's been ten times worse since she's been pregnant."

"Just like Duchess," said Mandy, remembering. "She got hit by a car when *she* was pregnant." Duchess was Delilah's mother. The accident had caused her to go into premature labor — luckily both Duchess and all her kittens had survived. She belonged to Richard Tanner, one of Mandy's and James's friends in the village. James let Tara go and the happy dog bounced over to Mandy to say hello. Mandy made a fuss over her and received a lick on the nose. Mandy grinned and scratched Tara's ears. "How are you going to like the kittens, Tara?"

Jane raised her eyebrows. "We hope she's going to get along fine with them, but we'll keep her away from them at first, at least until they're old enough to cope with her bounciness. We were going to ask your dad about the best way to introduce them. Bill's planning to bring Delilah to the clinic for another checkup tonight."

"Oh, good," said Mandy, straightening up and looking pleased. "I'll see her then."

Jane nodded. "And you must both come and see the kittens when they are born. It's good for kittens to have visitors." She smiled. "Anyway, I'd better let you two get off to school or you'll be late. Thanks again." She called to Tara. The dog bounded happily inside.

Mandy and James turned back down the path and the

door shut behind them. "Well, that turned out all right," said James, relieved. "Now I've just got to see if my bike's still working."

Mandy nodded but she was only half listening. A slight movement in the hedge had caught her eye. What was it? It looked like an animal. She frowned.

"Earth to Mandy!" said James, waving a hand in front of her face.

Mandy brushed him away and stopped. "Look," she said, in a low voice. "Over there in the hedge. It's a cat."

James frowned. "Where? I can't see anything."

"There," Mandy insisted, pointing.

James peered at the hedge. A short-haired tabby cat was lying watching them. Her brown-and-black fur blended in perfectly with the shadows. Her ears twitched warily. Her sleek, round body was tense.

Mandy held out her hand and approached quietly. "Here, puss. There's a good cat." She wondered what the cat was doing in the Wards' yard and why she looked so nervous. The cat crouched even farther into the ground. Now she was closer, Mandy could see that the cat's left ear was torn. Dark clots of dried blood were caked around the nasty wound. Mandy edged closer but it was too close for the cat. Leaping up, it raced across the grass and scrambled clumsily through the far hedge.

"Oh," said Mandy, watching it go.

James came over. "Do you know who it belongs to?"

Mandy shook her head. "I've never seen it before."

"An animal you don't know!" said James, grinning. "A miracle!"

Mandy didn't grin back. Her blue eyes looked rather worried. "Did you see its ear? It was torn. I think it's a stray."

"It can't be a stray," James argued. "It looked fat. It probably belongs to someone new in the village," he continued. "That's why you haven't seen it before."

"But why did it run away like that?" As they reached the road, Mandy looked in the direction the cat had gone.

"Oh, no!" James said, recognizing the look on Mandy's face. "You're not going after her. We're going to be late enough for school as it is!"

There was no sign of the little tabby cat so, rather reluctantly, Mandy picked up her bike. James's bike had survived the crash with only a few scrapes on the paintwork and a dent in the bell. They cycled off. James chatted away but Mandy was quiet almost all the way. She was thinking about the cat.

James was right, it *had* looked well fed. But if it belonged to someone, then why hadn't they done something about its ear and why had it looked so nervous? For some reason, she couldn't get the picture of the little cat scrambling through the hedge out of her mind. Something bothered her. It wasn't just its torn ear or the nervous look in its eyes. It was something else. But try as she might she couldn't figure out quite what.

Mandy slowed down as she and James cycled back past the Wards' house on their way home from school, her eyes sweeping across the neat yards and hedges.

"It's probably sitting safe and sound at home," said James, glancing at her. Mandy looked at him in surprise. He grinned. "You were looking for the tabby cat, weren't you?"

Mandy returned the grin. James knew her so well, sometimes it was as though he could read her thoughts. "But what if it hasn't got a home?"

"If it was a stray it would have been skinnier," James pointed out.

Mandy nodded, but deep down she still wasn't convinced. They cycled on until they reached the point in the village where they separated. "See you tomorrow!" she called.

A few minutes later, she turned up the driveway that led to Animal Ark. The veterinary clinic was a modern extension at the back of the old stone cottage where the Hopes lived. Leaving her bike leaning against the clinic wall, Mandy went into the waiting room.

Jean Knox, the Animal Ark receptionist, was sitting behind the desk. Her glasses dangled on a chain as she poked cautiously at the computer keyboard. "How was school?" she asked, looking up as Mandy came in.

"Okay," Mandy replied. She frowned. "Jean, do you know if anyone's moved into the village with a brown tabby cat?"

Jean shook her head and started tapping with one finger on the keyboard again. "I haven't heard of anyone. Why?"

Mandy explained. "It didn't look thin but it had a torn ear and wouldn't come near me."

Simon, the practical nurse, came out of one of the treatment rooms. He had been at Animal Ark since leaving college and was good friends with Mandy. She asked him the same question.

He thought for a moment but then shook his head. "Can't help you, I'm afraid," he said, running a hand through his short blond hair. "Maybe your mom or dad will know."

"Where are they?" Mandy asked Jean as Simon returned to the treatment room with some medical powder.

"Your mom's out on a farm visit and your dad's with Mrs. Platt," Jean informed her.

"Antonia's all right, isn't she?" Mandy asked. She was very fond of Mrs. Platt's little gray poodle.

Jean nodded. "Just in for her kennel cough vaccination and some medicine."

The clinic door opened and in walked Bill Ward, carrying a wicker cat basket. Mandy hurried over. "Hi! How's Delilah?"

The mailman smiled. "She's grand," he said, putting the basket down on one of the seats. "Jane told me about you and James this morning." He nodded. "Thanks, dear."

"That's all right," said Mandy. "As long as she's safe."

"Sounds interesting," said a deep, warm voice. Mandy swung around. Her father had come through from the treatment room with Mrs. Platt and was listening to the conversation. His mouth crinkled at the corners under his beard. "What have you been up to now?"

Mandy told him about the near accident that morning.

"Delilah just loves running across that road," Bill Ward said to Dr. Adam.

"Bring her in," said Dr. Adam with a smile. He looked at Mandy. "Are you coming in, too?"

"Yes, please."

Now that she was twelve, Mandy was allowed to help with the animals that came in to the clinic. She cleaned out the cages, helped with the medication, and assisted in the treatment room. It could be hard work but she loved it. She took her white coat down off the peg and, buttoning it up, hurried to join her dad and Mr. Ward in the treatment room. Delilah was sitting on the rubber-topped table.

Dr. Adam ran his hands gently over her bulging sides. "Not long to go now," he said, looking up at Bill Ward. "Have you gotten her a nesting box?"

Bill nodded, his green eyes serious. "Just a cardboard box with a lid. It's all ready in the living room and she's been going in and ripping up the newspaper we put inside." He stroked Delilah's head and looked down fondly at her. "We're looking forward to these kittens."

"Excellent," said Dr. Adam. He looked in Delilah's eyes and mouth and then parted the dense white hair on her back and inspected the skin. "No sign of fleas," he said. "But make sure you comb her daily. Can you pass me the thermometer, please, Mandy?"

Mandy held Delilah while her father took Delilah's temperature and then listened to her heart. "Yes, everything seems normal," he said. "She's in fine condition, Bill."

"She should be," said Bill Ward. "She's on four meals a day. Best minced chicken, fish, and liver, twice a week. We've got to keep up her strength." Carefully, he put Delilah back into her basket.

Mandy helped him to do up the straps. She wondered

if he knew anything about the tabby cat in his yard. "When James and I were at your house this morning we saw another cat in your yard," she said. "It was a tabby cat. Do you know if it belongs to anyone?"

"Sure, I know the one you mean. I'm pretty sure she's a stray," Bill Ward said as Dr. Adam reached for the disinfectant spray and started to wipe down the table to make it ready for the next animal. "I've caught sight of her a few times. Yesterday, I came out on my way to work and found her lying under the cherry tree. Seeing her condition, I tried to catch her but she was off like a shot as soon as I got near."

"Condition? You mean her ear?" Mandy frowned. "Yes, I was worried about that."

Bill looked surprised. "Ear? Her ears looked okay yesterday." He shook his head. "No, I mean about her being pregnant."

"Pregnant!" Mandy stared.

"Yes. As soon as I saw her I could tell. She was like Delilah, licking her flanks — with her belly bulging in just the same way. I'd recognize those signs anywhere at the moment."

Mandy's blue eyes widened as she realized what had been bothering her. James had said the cat looked fat but the fat had been all to the side and underneath. She thought of the clumsy way the cat had pushed through the hedge. It wasn't well fed — it was pregnant!

She turned anxiously to her father. "Do you think she'll be all right?"

Dr. Adam scratched his beard. "Cats normally have kittens without too much problem. But we should probably catch her and take her up to the Animal Sanctuary. She may need feeding up and then there'll be kittens who need homes."

Bill Ward nodded. "I put some food out after she ran off. She doesn't look like she's had much to eat recently."

Mandy was very concerned. She knew that it got harder for female cats to hunt when they were pregnant. The poor thing was probably half starving. She remembered the way its big green eyes had stared at her. "When can we go, Dad?"

"I've got appointments for the rest of the day," Dr. Adam said. "And then I'm on call." He turned to Bill. "You said you usually see her in the morning?"

The other man nodded.

"Well, would it be all right if we came to your house to see if she's there? If she is, we can catch her and take her to the Animal Sanctuary."

"Of course, but it will have to be early," said Bill. "I start my mail round at seven."

"So if we come about six o'clock?" Dr. Adam suggested.

"I'll be there," said Bill. "I wouldn't bet on your chances of catching her, though," he said, scratching his head. "Not the way she ran off when I tried to get near."

Two

"Well, here we are," said Dr. Adam, drawing the Land Rover up outside the Wards' house the following morning. "Now, let's see if we can find this cat."

Mandy opened the back of the Land Rover. *I hope she's here*, she thought as she lifted out a plastic cat carrier and a bowl of food. She frowned. What would they do if she wasn't?

She joined her father in the Wards' yard. The grass was heavy with dew, each blade sparkling in the rays of the early morning sun. Dr. Adam scratched his beard. "I can't see her."

Mandy's eyes searched the hedges and borders but

there was no sign of the cat. Her heart sank. "Maybe Mr. Ward has seen her," she suggested. "She might have been here and left already."

She was halfway down the path toward the front door when she suddenly froze. "There!" she gasped in a low voice. "Dad! Look! By the shed!"

The tabby cat lay in the mottled shadows of Bill Ward's outdoor shed, her brown-and-black coat providing the perfect camouflage. Now, Mandy could see how thin she really was. Her stomach bulged, but her face was gaunt and her backbone stuck out.

"She certainly looks pregnant," said Dr. Adam, quietly coming up behind Mandy. "Let's see if we can get near." He took a couple of steps toward the cat. Her ears pricked. Her green eyes widened. "Put the food down, Mandy," Dr. Adam said softly. Mandy took a step closer and reached out with the bowl, but the movement was too much for the cat. Turning on the spot, she raced around the side of the cottage.

Mandy saw the concern on her father's face. "I think Bill was right. This isn't going to be easy," he said. "Let's give her time to settle down and then try again. Leave the food here. We'll see if Bill minds us watching from inside."

They walked up to the front door. Bill opened it. He had seen everything from the living-room window. "Jane's still in bed," he said. "But come and have a cup of tea while you wait," he said. "Watch out for Tara," he warned, pausing before opening the kitchen door. "She may jump up."

As soon as the door was opened, Tara flew at them like a canine cannonball. Mandy was thoroughly licked. Dr. Adam fended off the dog and when she had stopped jumping up, bent down to pat her. "Mad dog!" he laughed.

Delilah was curled up on one of the pine chairs, oblivious to the commotion. Mandy stroked her. She could feel the bulge of the kittens underneath the Persian's soft, dense fur. She looked so healthy. Mandy couldn't help thinking about the poor little cat outside who had no one to love her or take care of her.

They took mugs of tea into the living room where they could watch the front yard and the food bowl. Delilah lazily followed them through. She lay down and rolled on the rug, stretching herself out and arching her back luxuriantly. Tara sat down, leaning against Dr. Adam's legs and looking up at him with dark brown eyes that demanded attention.

"Is that Delilah's birthing box?" asked Mandy, pointing to a large cardboard box that stood by the radiator.

Bill nodded.

Mandy lifted the lid and looked inside. There were torn-up newspapers and soft paper towels lining the

bottom. At the front, Mr. Ward had cut a little door for Delilah to get in and out. "Will you take the lid off when she's having the kittens?" Mandy asked.

Bill nodded. "We'll keep a watchful eye on her."

"Now, call the clinic when she starts, won't you?" said Dr. Adam. "Persians can sometimes have problems giving birth because the kittens have quite large heads. I'd like to be here just to check that everything is okay."

Mandy glanced out of the window. The tabby cat was creeping cautiously across the lawn, her wary eyes looking from side to side as she approached the bowl of food. "Dad! It's the cat!"

Dr. Adam stood up and looked out of the window. "I'll go out the back door," he said. "Mandy, you go out the front. Careful now, remember it's very important that we don't upset her. The kittens would probably be too young to survive if she gave birth now."

Her heart beating fast, Mandy opened the front door. The cat looked at her and then, putting its head down, carried on eating, gulping the food as fast as she could.

Mandy started to walk slowly toward it, her feet making prints in the dew. Out of the corner of her eye she could see her dad coming up from the other direction. He was crouching down and holding a tasty treat. Mandy edged closer.

The cat stopped eating.

"There now," Mandy soothed. "We're not going to hurt you. It's all right."

The cat turned to run but came face-to-face with Dr. Adam holding out the treat. For one hope-filled moment, Mandy thought the little cat was going to be tempted by the tidbit, but the next instant the tabby had changed her mind and, swerving across the grass, scrambled away through the hedge.

Mandy watched in dismay. "Now what are we going to do?"

Dr. Adam sighed and heaved himself up off the grass. "Give up," he said, wiping the grass off his trousers.

Mandy stared at him in horror. "Dad, we can't! You saw how thin the poor thing was. She needs looking after!"

Dr. Adam put his hand gently on Mandy's shoulder. "We can't risk upsetting her any more, Mandy," he said. "We'd be putting the unborn kittens in danger." Dr. Adam turned to Bill Ward. "She seems to have taken a liking to your yard. If she comes back, do you think you can leave some food out for her first thing in the morning and last thing at night? I think we'll have to try to win her trust and hope that, after a few days, she'll let us get close enough to help."

Bill Ward nodded. "No problem."

Relief overwhelmed Mandy. She gave her dad a hug.

She should have known he wouldn't let her down. "Can I help?" she asked eagerly.

"Well, if Bill doesn't object," Dr. Adam said, glancing inquiringly in Bill's direction, "I suggest that you and James come and leave some food for the cat each day on your way to and from school."

"It's fine by me," said Bill cheerfully.

Mandy's blue eyes shone. "We can wait while she eats," she said eagerly. "If she sees us here and realizes we're not going to hurt her, maybe, after a bit, she'll let us go up to her."

Dr. Adam raised his eyebrows. "That sounds like an ideal excuse for being late for school, Mandy Hope."

"We'll get here early," promised Mandy. "We'll be here by seven."

Dr. Adam's eyes twinkled. "And what will James say about that?"

Mandy grinned. Her dad knew how much James hated getting up early. "He'll moan at first but he won't really mind. You'll see!"

"Seven o'clock!" exclaimed James as they biked to school. "That means getting up at . . ." he did a rapid calculation in his head, ". . . at quarter past *six*!" He stared at Mandy incredulously.

"It's not for long," said Mandy. "Just until the cat starts letting us near her."

"Well, I guess it is in a good cause," James grumbled.

"You know it is," said Mandy. Her head was buzzing with excitement. In her schoolbag was a tin of cat food, a fork, a bowl, and some vitamin tablets that her father had given her before she left Animal Ark. "She's bound to get used to us if we're there when she's eating, and then we'll be able to catch her and take care of her."

"When do you think she'll have her kittens?" asked James. "She's not quite as big as Delilah yet, is she?"

"But she hasn't had all the food Delilah's had," Mandy pointed out. "And anyway, Delilah will look larger because of her fluffy hair. Maybe the kittens are due quite soon." She frowned. "I wonder where she came from? Maybe we should put up some notices."

James nodded. "We could ask if we could do them on the school computer at lunchtime and put them up on the way home."

After school, they took the notices they had printed out around to some of the shops in Walton. "We can do the ones in Welford after we've fed the cat," said Mandy as they came out of the Walton bookstore. "There's the post office and Animal Ark, of course, and maybe

Mr. Hardy would let us put one up in the *Fox and Goose*."

The wind whipped about their faces as they cycled home. It was a cold day but Mandy hardly noticed. Her mind was fixed on the cat. Would she be in the Wards' yard? Mandy pedaled extra quickly up the last hill, free-wheeling down it, and screeching to a stop outside the Wards' house. James stopped beside her a few seconds later.

"I'm glad we don't have cats to feed every day!" he gasped, pushing his hair out of his eyes and readjusting his glasses.

Mandy grinned. "You know you want to see if she's there just as much as I do. Come on!"

As they unlatched the gate, Mrs. Ward came hurrying out of the front door. "I'm just popping into Walton," she said to them. "Bill told me about the poor little thing. Imagine it being pregnant like Delilah."

"Have you seen her today?" Mandy asked.

"She was by the shed when I got back from work about ten minutes ago," Mrs. Ward said. "I put some water out for her. I've been keeping Tara in the backyard so as not to disturb her."

Mandy and James put down their bags. "We'll put the food in the same place," said Mandy. James got out the bowl from Mandy's backpack and Mandy forked the food into it. There was no sign of the cat. They sat down on the front porch and watched. Mandy shivered in the cold air and pulled her coat around her.

"There!" whispered James, nudging her gently with his elbow. "Look!" The tabby cat came slinking along under the cover of the hedge. She edged toward the food, took a nervous look around, and plunged her head into the bowl. Her sides moved in and out as she gulped the food down. "Look how her ribs stick out!" Mandy said.

At the sound of Mandy's voice the cat's head shot up. Her green eyes stared warily in the direction of the porch. Mandy froze. Oh, no, why had she spoken? She held her breath. There was a long pause and then the cat slowly lowered her head and continued to devour the food.

The breath rushed out of Mandy. She exchanged relieved looks with James, but neither of them dared say another word until the cat had finished and trotted off across the garden and under the hedge.

As they washed the bowl at the outside tap, James said, "We should bring her some milk. Eric loves milk." Eric was James's young cat.

Mandy looked a bit doubtful. "Some adult cats are allergic to cow's milk," she said, remembering an article she had read in one of her dad's magazines. "It can make them really sick." She frowned. "But pregnant cats need calcium and milk is a really good source. Maybe we *should* give it a try." Her eyes suddenly brightened. "I've got an idea! The article said cats that are allergic to cow's milk can normally drink goat's milk."

James looked at her. "Lydia!" he exclaimed.

"Exactly!" said Mandy with a grin.

Lydia Fawcett kept goats at High Cross Farm, a small farm set up on the hills outside the village. She was great friends with Mandy and James and would be sure to let them have some of her goats' milk.

Throwing the bowl and vitamin tablets into Mandy's backpack, the two friends set off on their bikes for High Cross Farm. It was a long climb uphill, past the iron gates of Beacon House where the Parker-Smythes lived, past the tall evergreen hedges that hid Upper Welford Hall, and then a bumpy ride along an unpaved road.

They finally reached the new five-barred gate that marked the entrance to High Cross Farm. Pushing it open they wheeled their bikes up the path to the stone farmhouse.

"It's all looking much better than it used to," said James, looking at the freshly painted red door of the house and the recently repaired outbuildings.

"It must be from all the money that the milk's bringing in," said Mandy, pleased. At one time, Lydia had been very hard up, but Mandy and James had helped her to make a profit from the farm by persuading local health food shops to buy Lydia's goats' milk and cheese.

Lydia Fawcett came marching around the side of the barn. She was dressed in old knee boots and a tattered jacket. Her weather-beaten face crinkled into a smile when she saw Mandy and James. "Why, this is a nice surprise," she said, striding over. "What brings the pair of you up here? Have you just come to see the goats or are you here for something in particular?"

Mandy explained about the tabby cat and their attempts to fill her up. "So you see," she concluded, "we thought goat's milk might be good for her."

"It'll be just the thing," said Lydia, nodding approvingly. "Best milk in the world."

"Particularly from High Cross Farm goats," said James with a grin.

Lydia jerked her head toward the dairy. "Come on, I'll fetch you some. You can say hello to old Houdini on the way." She stomped off up the path. They followed her, passing a field with a very high chain-link fence. On the other side of the fence stood a beautiful black goat with intelligent green eyes.

"Houdini!" said Mandy. He blinked at her and let her

stroke him through the wire. "Has he escaped recently?" Mandy asked Lydia. Houdini had been given his name because he was very good at escaping.

Lydia shook her head. "No more escaping for him, the old scoundrel," she said. "Not with that fence. But Henry seems to be taking after him." Henry was Houdini's young son. "He's already gotten out of his field a few times."

In the dairy, Lydia handed them three cartons of goat's milk.

"Thanks, Lydia," Mandy said gratefully. "It's really kind of you."

Lydia coughed and looked embarrassed. "Well, you've helped me enough in the past," she said, rather gruffly. "It's my turn to repay the favor. Just you come back whenever you want some more."

Mandy and James put the cartons in the backpack, said a quick hello to the other goats, and then set off back down the hill to put out some goat's milk for the tabby.

When Mandy got back to Animal Ark, she put on her white coat and went through to the residential unit to see what animals were in that night. She found her mother changing a dressing on the leg of an English bullterrier. "Hi, honey," Dr. Emily said, looking up with a smile.

Mandy hurried over. "Do you want some help?"

"Thanks. This young chap got caught in some barbed wire." Dr. Emily held a new dressing firmly against the wound. "Can you pass me a bandage?" Mandy did as her mom asked and stood ready to pass the scissors and tape. Dr. Emily worked quickly and skillfully. Mandy stroked the dog's white face. He was still sleepy from the anesthetic. "There, he should be good as new when that heals up." Dr. Emily cut the end of the tape and straightened up, brushing back a long strand of red hair that had escaped from the knot at the base of her neck. "Now then, how was your day?" she asked Mandy.

As Mandy made the dog comfortable in his cage, she told her mother all about the tabby cat and the notices she and James had put up.

"Hopefully *someone* will know who the cat belongs to," Mandy said.

Dr. Emily looked up from clearing away the dressing. "She might have been abandoned."

Mandy nodded. "She doesn't seem to like people very much."

"Have you thought of a name for her?" Dr. Emily asked.

Mandy shook her head. Up to now she had just been thinking of the little tabby as "the cat." She ran through names in her head. Tabby . . . Tabitha . . . Socks . . . Whiskers. None of them seemed quite right. "I'll ask James tomorrow," she said.

Dr. Emily smiled. "Can you finish up in here? I'll put some supper on for us. Your dad's out helping with a lambing at Fordbeck Farm."

She left Mandy to wipe down the surfaces and settle the animals. As well as the bullterrier, there was a rabbit recovering from an operation to remove a lodged fur ball and a gerbil with suspected vitamin C deficiency. As Mandy worked, she thought about possible names for the cat. The bullterrier whimpered in his cage. Mandy crouched down beside him and soothed him until he went to sleep.

At last, convinced that he was happily settled, she got to her feet. "Good night," she whispered softly and quietly shut the door.

When James came for Mandy at ten to seven the next morning, she had already been up for nearly an hour. She had cleaned out the cages in the residential unit and talked to the patients, all of whom were looking a bit better.

She dashed into the kitchen. Dr. Adam was eating a plate of scrambled eggs. The Fordbeck Farm lambing had been followed by another call later in the evening, and he was looking tired and bleary-eyed.

"Sit down and have some breakfast," Dr. Emily said to Mandy.

But Mandy could hear James's bike coming up the drive. She grabbed a banana and a cereal bar from the side. "See you later!"

"Mandy, have some breakfast!" But Mandy was out of the door, leaving her mother staring despairingly after her.

James's brown hair was tousled and he still looked half asleep. "It's too early!" he grumbled.

Mandy grinned. "Your sweater's on backward." James looked down. "Come on!" said Mandy, leaping on her bike. "You can change it at the Wards'." She pedaled off down the drive.

"You know, we should think of a name for the cat," Mandy said as James caught up.

"Tabby?" suggested James.

Mandy shook her head. "Too boring. What about Socks?"

James shook his head. "Sounds like a boy." They biked through the quiet streets, exchanging names, but couldn't seem to agree on anything. They passed Bill Ward's van parked by the post office on the main street. It was seven o'clock and he was just about to start work.

"Should we knock on the door and let Mrs. Ward know we're here or just put the food out?" James wondered as they arrived at the Wards' house.

"Just put the food out," decided Mandy. "Mrs. Ward might be getting ready for work and it will only make Tara bark if we knock. They know we're coming." She left her bike against the hedge and looked over the gate. "Look!" she breathed, grabbing James's arm as he moved to unlatch the gate.

There, lying on the grass under the cherry tree, was the tabby cat. She rolled lazily onto her back, her tail swishing through the fallen blossoms. She rubbed her head and body into the ground, luxuriating in it. Clawing up a clump of blossoms, she pushed it up into the air. It fluttered down around her and she batted at it with her paw. Mandy realized it was the first time she had ever seen the little cat look happy.

She turned to James, her eyes shining. "Blossom!" she whispered. "We'll call her Blossom."

James nodded and grinned.

Blossom eventually got up and shook herself. She trotted a short distance away and sat down to groom her flanks. Mandy and James entered the yard as quietly as they could.

"Let's go straight past her," Mandy said in a low voice. "Don't even look at her." They walked quietly past and dished out the food. James poured out the goat's milk into a saucer. Putting the things back in their bag, they went quietly to the porch, taking care to stay far away from the little cat.

She had stopped grooming and was watching them intently. They sat on the porch and, keeping one wary eye on them, she trotted to the food bowl. "At least she hasn't run away," said James. He smiled at Mandy. "Blossom's a good name. It suits her."

Blossom gulped down every morsel of food, lapped up the milk, and then, trotting a short distance away, sat down to clean her face and whiskers. Mandy looked at the swell of the little cat's belly. "You know, I think she's expecting her kittens quite soon. She's not all that different in shape from Delilah."

"Oh, she is," James disagreed. "I bet it's going to be a while." But Mandy wasn't so sure.

Leaving Blossom to snooze off her breakfast, they crept out of the yard. Mandy stopped for one last look at the little cat. "Bye, Blossom," she said softly. The cat pricked up her ears. Mandy stared at her. It was as though Blossom had recognized her name.

*   *   *

As the week passed, Blossom slowly seemed to accept Mandy and James's presence in the yard. By the end of the week, they could get to almost within a few feet without her running off, but she still wouldn't let them get close enough to touch her.

Mandy became impatient. She wanted to pick Blossom up and check her over and clean up her ear. The one consolation was that the wound seemed to be healing itself, and she was sure that Blossom's ribs were sticking out a little less than they had done before. *Softly, softly*, she kept telling herself firmly. *If we rush too close too soon it could spoil everything.*

On Friday, when they stopped at the Wards' after school, Blossom was nowhere to be seen but Bill Ward was standing by the shed, peering inside. He looked around as they opened the gate. He beckoned them over to the shed, one finger held up to his lips, warning them to keep quiet.

Mandy and James exchanged puzzled looks but hurried over. "Look," said Bill. "Look in here." He eased the door open a little wider. Mandy peered inside. It was dim in the shed after the brightness of outside, and at first she couldn't see anything apart from tools, plant pots, and gardening equipment.

Bill nodded toward one of the back corners. Mandy's

eyes widened. There, sitting at the back of the shed, in an old tin bath lined with bits of newspaper, was Blossom!

"She's preparing for birthing," Bill said. "I saw her going in the shed once or twice yesterday. This afternoon I kept watch and there she was, nesting in that old tub. She'd dragged in an old piece of cloth I kept for wiping my hands on." He smiled. "I was keeping that tub to put geraniums in this summer but I guess it's got a better use now. I stuck a layer of newspaper in this afternoon when she left for a bit."

Blossom stared at them. She seemed wary and cautious, but it was a far cry from the blind panic she had shown when Dr. Adam and Mandy had first tried to get near. "Let's put the food down in here," Mandy said softly.

She and James quickly sorted out the food and then slipped it halfway between the shed door and the tub. They stood back. Would Blossom come and eat it? Blossom didn't move. Mandy felt disappointed. Blossom had been letting them get that close to her in the yard.

"Better leave her to it," said Bill. "She'll eat when we're gone."

"Maybe it's because she's in the shed," James said quietly to Mandy as they slipped out the door. "I'm sure she would have come if we'd been outside."

Mandy looked at him gratefully. He always knew the right things to say to make her feel better. As they packed away the empty tin and dirty spoon, Mandy had a sudden thought. "If she's nesting, then that must mean she's about to have her kittens."

Bill Ward scratched his chin. "Delilah's been nesting for going on two weeks now. I think Blossom's got a while to go yet."

"Can we see Delilah?" James asked.

"Of course. Come on in," Bill replied.

Mandy and James followed him into the house. Tara shot out of her basket when she saw them. Her tail thwacked against the table and the cupboards as she jumped around their legs. Mandy rubbed her ears and scratched under her chin.

"Delilah's in the living room," said Mr. Ward. "Go through if you want but shut the door so Tara can't get in. She's a scoundrel for jumping on the furniture."

James held Tara back as Mandy slipped into the living room and then he nimbly whizzed through the door, shutting it in Tara's disappointed face. "Sorry, girl, but we're here to see Delilah!"

Delilah was walking around the living room. Mandy reached down to stroke her, but Delilah shrugged her off and continued pacing. She was breathing heavily.

Her sides were moving in and out. Opening her mouth, she emitted a sharp cry.

"What's the matter with her?" James asked in alarm.

Mandy didn't reply. She was staring at the cat. A movement rippled through Delilah's body.

"James!" she gasped suddenly. "Get Mr. Ward. I think Delilah's about to have her kittens!"

Three

"You're right!" Bill Ward stared at Delilah. Another contraction rippled through the cat. "We better see if she'll go into her box."

"Why isn't she in there already?" asked James.

"Sometimes they like to pace," said Bill. "Particularly when it's their first time like Delilah here. But looking at her, I'd say she hasn't long to go now."

He took the lid off the box and gently encouraged Delilah through the door. "Come on then, pet. It's time you came in here." The cat walked slowly into her box.

"Should I call Animal Ark?" asked Mandy.

"The phone's in the kitchen," said Bill, nodding.

Mandy dialed the number and spoke to Jean, who promised to send Dr. Adam along right away. Mandy returned to the living room. "Dad will be here soon," she said.

"Is there anything we can do?" James asked anxiously as Delilah groaned rather alarmingly.

"She's doing just fine," Bill said calmly. "The kittens will be some time yet. There's a box of towels ready in the kitchen. You could get those — and while you're in there, stick the kettle on and I'll make us all a cup of tea." James hurried off, carefully shutting the kitchen door after him so Tara couldn't come through and bother Delilah.

"Have you raised many litters of kittens?" Mandy asked Bill.

He nodded. "When I was a kid. Delilah's my first for a while, though, and also my first pedigree. Still, having kittens doesn't change as far as I can tell." He looked at Delilah. "I think she'll be another half hour yet." He smiled at them. "Are you and James going to stay and watch?"

"I'd love to," said Mandy.

"Can I call my mom, please?" asked James, coming through with the towels. "I should tell her where I am if we're going to be here a while."

Bill nodded and James hurried back through to the kitchen.

They were sitting around Delilah's box when Dr. Adam arrived. "So how's the mother-to-be?" he asked, coming in and looking into the box. He gently examined Delilah. "Ah, good, it all looks like it's going according to plan. The first kitten's almost here. Headfirst presentation. Excellent."

Delilah sat up. Mandy could see the head emerging. She watched as a tiny white kitten eased out. Its eyes were tightly shut. Its coat was damp. Delilah started to lick roughly at its face. The kitten opened its mouth and took its first breath.

"Oh!" said Mandy. "Isn't it wonderful!" She had seen many animals being born, and had even helped in some cases, but the wonder of it never ceased for her. She looked at her father, her eyes shining.

"Nothing ever beats seeing a healthy animal born," he said softly.

Mandy looked at Delilah cleaning her firstborn. It was at times like this that Mandy knew that there was nothing in the world that she wanted more than to be a vet.

James peered rather cautiously into the box, but when he saw the tiny kitten with Delilah he smiled, too.

"How many more will there be?" Mandy asked her father.

"Persians don't normally have very large litters, probably only three or four," Dr. Adam replied.

They waited. Jane Ward arrived home from work and came to join them. After a bit, Delilah started to push again. Out came a second kitten, then a third, and then a fourth. All white. All coming into the world easily and with no complications. After the fourth kitten had been licked clean, Delilah started to clean herself and the box.

"Well, that looks like it might be it," said Dr. Adam. "And she didn't need us at all." The kittens cuddled into Delilah as she settled back and started to let them feed. They lay in a row, their little tails sticking straight out behind, their heads buried in their mother's soft fur.

Mandy looked at Delilah and her four healthy kittens. She sighed happily.

"Well, we better get home," said Dr. Adam, starting to stand up. "Do you want a lift, James? We can throw the bikes in the back."

"Yes, please." James and Dr. Adam started to help clear away the empty mugs.

"I'll go and get Blossom's feeding bowl," said Mandy, seizing the chance to take another quick look at the tabby cat. "It will be easier to wash it out tonight."

She slipped out the back door. It was cool outside and almost dark. The light from the kitchen lit up the path to the shed. She gently opened the door and peered into the shadows. It was difficult to see. She opened the door wider to let in more light. Yes, there was Blossom, lying in the old tin bath.

Mandy stiffened. Something dark and small was lying beside her. She stared. What was it? She picked her way past plant pots and garden tools. Her foot clanged against a metal bucket and she stumbled over a bag of fertilizer, but the tabby cat hardly even looked up. Mandy reached the tub. Her eyes widened. Lying beside Blossom was a tiny, damp kitten!

The sudden grin of delight on Mandy's face faded as quickly as it had come. Why wasn't Blossom looking after her kitten? She wasn't licking it or nursing it. Mandy swallowed hard, worry clutching her stomach. It wasn't dead, was it?

Her heart thudded. To her utter relief she saw the kitten move slightly. It was alive! The breath escaped from Mandy in a rush. She looked at Blossom and frowned. She was lying very still, not like Delilah. Delilah had been restless, moving around, changing position, seeing to the kittens.

Blossom rested her head on the newspaper. Mandy suddenly had the feeling that something was wrong, badly wrong. Blossom needed help!

Dr. Adam was talking to the Wards in the kitchen when Mandy flung open the door. She stopped in the doorway, her blue eyes wide in her pale face. "Quick!" she gasped. Everyone looked up in surprise.

"What's the matter?" Dr. Adam asked, looking at her with concern.

"It's Blossom!" Mandy urged. "She's having her kittens but I think something's the matter!"

Mandy turned and raced back to the shed. The others hurried after her. Bill Ward grabbed a flashlight from a shelf by the back door. Its powerful beam of light cut through the gloom. Blossom still lay motionless. Dr.

Adam took one look and then quickly started to clear a path through the boxes and pots. "Mandy. Get my bag, please. It's in the kitchen."

Mandy hurried into the house. Bill dug out a lamp from the shed. He hung it on a hook so Dr. Adam could see clearly. James and Jane helped to clear a path through the gardening equipment.

"What's the matter with her?" asked Mandy, as her dad leaned over and examined Blossom.

"Uterine inertia," said Dr. Adam grimly, straightening up.

James looked at Mandy for a clue as to what uterine inertia was but Mandy didn't know, either. Rummaging through his bag, Dr. Adam explained. "It means that the mother cat has stopped having contractions even though there are more kittens to come out. I think there must be another kitten blocking the way. I can give her an injection to get the contractions going again, but before I do that I need to find out if there is a blockage and what's causing it."

"Should we move her inside?" asked Jane, looking worried.

Dr. Adam shook his head. "It might upset her. But if you can find any more light that would be good. I'll need some of those towels you had ready for Delilah. And a hot-water bottle and a small cardboard box. I think kitten number one looks like it is going to need some help."

Jane hurried off to the house. Mandy and James watched Blossom anxiously, counting the minutes that Jane was away.

Finally she returned, her hands full. Dr. Adam picked up the kitten. "Still alive," he murmured, turning to Jane. "Can I have a towel?" She handed him one and Dr. Adam rubbed it firmly over the kitten. He looked at Mandy. "Mandy, can you take over with this? I need to start on Blossom."

"Sure," said Mandy eagerly. She reached out and her dad placed the tiny kitten gently in her hands. "Rub it with the towel," he told her. "When it's dry put it in the cardboard box. James, can you get the new box ready? It needs a layer of newspaper and then the hot-water bottle wrapped in a towel. We'll put the kittens in there."

Mandy and James got busy with their tasks as Dr. Adam started to examine Blossom. The damp kitten in the palm of Mandy's hand was tiny. She rubbed it firmly. "Come on," she breathed, holding it close to her face. "You're going to be all right."

"I was right," Dr. Adam said at last. "There is a kitten stuck. It's in the worst position. Head turned around."

"Can you move it?" asked Mandy, looking up anxiously from rubbing the kitten.

Dr. Adam's face was serious. "I'll try. It's really our only hope. Blossom's so weak and undernourished I doubt she could survive an operation."

"What about the kitten inside?" James asked, putting the cardboard box next to Mandy. "Will it be okay?"

"It depends how long it's been there," said Dr. Adam. "There's a limit to the length of time a kitten can survive like that. We might well be too late."

Mandy's heart sank. She placed the first tiny kitten in the box and covered it up. It was dry now and she knew it needed the heat from the hot-water bottle. She watched anxiously as her dad tried to help Blossom, his face set with concentration.

Time dragged by. Mandy felt close to tears. *Poor, poor little Blossom.* Dr. Adam was a brilliant vet, one of the best, but Mandy knew the harsh realities of a vet's life. Sometimes, being brilliant wasn't enough.

"I can't get it around," Dr. Adam muttered.

Fingers of despair curled around Mandy's heart. Bill Ward looked on, a deeply worried look on his normally cheerful face.

Dr. Adam shook his head. "No, it's not coming . . . yes!" he suddenly exclaimed. "It's there!"

He straightened up. "It's turned."

"Oh, Dad!" gasped Mandy. "Well done!"

Dr. Adam reached for a syringe in his bag and injected Blossom. "Now the contractions should start again."

Mandy leaned forward. "Is the kitten still alive?"

Dr. Adam shrugged. "We'll just have to wait and see."

The injection started to work its magic. Gradually, contractions started to ripple through Blossom's sides. Mandy crossed her fingers. The second kitten started to appear. It slithered out, headfirst, onto the paper. Everyone held their breath as Blossom started to nose it and lick it. She cleaned its face and nostrils but the kitten lay still.

"Too late," muttered Bill, shaking his head.

Mandy's mouth went dry. She looked at her father. He was leaning forward with a speculative look in his eyes, peering at the ginger kitten. Hope flickered through her. "Dad?" Mandy faltered. *Had he seen something?* And then she saw it, too. The kitten moved. Everyone gasped. "It's alive!" Mandy cried.

Blossom started to clean the kitten vigorously. James pushed a relieved hand through his tousled hair. Bill put his arm around Jane's shoulders and hugged her. "Not too late after all," said Dr. Adam, smiling at Mandy.

Mandy's legs suddenly felt wobbly. The kitten had

survived. Both mother and baby had been saved. She watched in delight as Blossom gave birth to one more kitten and immediately began licking it. "I think that's all of them," said Dr. Adam, watching Blossom finish cleaning the kitten and then herself. The two little kittens beside her pushed through her fur toward nourishment. Dr. Adam picked them up one by one and looked at them. "It's always easiest to tell what they are when they are newborn," he explained to the watchers. "The ginger one's obviously a boy. The tabby's a girl."

Mandy picked up the cardboard box. "What about this one?"

Dr. Adam took the tabby-and-white kitten out of the cardboard box and examined her quickly. "Another girl," he said with a smile, placing her carefully next to the rest. Blossom settled back happily to let her three babies feed.

As everyone left the shed, Mandy lingered for one moment more to look at the sleeping kittens. A warm glow of happiness spread through her.

Two mothers. Seven kittens.

What an evening!

Four

The next morning, Mandy and James bumped along the track to High Cross Farm. The sun was shining brightly but the wind on the hillside was cold and Mandy was glad to have her gloves. She inhaled deeply. She loved this time of year, everything growing, the fields clothed in fresh, green grass, young animals being born.

She thought about the kittens at the Wards' house. She and James had stopped by there first thing, but the kittens and the two mother cats had all been asleep so they had decided to go up to High Cross Farm to fetch some more milk.

Leaving their bikes by the farmhouse, they went in search of Lydia. "Let's try the barn," said James, heading over to a long, low building. "She's probably in there."

They unlatched the heavy barn door and found Lydia cleaning out the goats' pens inside. "Morning," she said cheerily. "Come for some more milk?"

"If you don't mind," said Mandy.

Lydia looked surprised. "Of course not. I said to come anytime. You should know by now that I always mean what I say. Now, you might as well make yourself useful. I could do with some fresh straw over here."

Mandy grinned. Lydia could be a bit brusque sometimes but her heart was in the right place. Carrying the golden straw over, Mandy told Lydia all about the kittens. James stopped to stroke a small black goat in a pen near the door.

"Watch him!" Lydia warned. "He'll try to eat your sweater." James jumped back just in time. Lydia chuckled. "Henry will eat anything, the little rascal." She nodded at James. "Can you pass me that brush?"

Mandy and James busied themselves. The goats pushed against the bars of their pens, seeking attention.

There was the sudden clunk of a metal bolt drawing back. Mandy, James, and Lydia swung around. Henry was pulling back the bolt on his pen with his strong teeth.

"Quick! Stop him!" Mandy gasped to James as Henry pushed the pen door open with his nose.

James leaped toward the little black goat. With an excited bleat, Henry shot out of his pen and took off down the passageway.

"The main door's open!" James exclaimed. "I didn't lock it behind me!"

"Oh, no!" groaned Lydia.

The three of them started to run after Henry but it was too late. The little goat had reached the main door. He butted it open and leaped joyfully outside.

Mandy, James, and Lydia charged after him. His head held high, Henry trotted over to Houdini's field. He began to graze on the tufts of grass growing outside the enclosure.

"Come on, Henry. Come here," coaxed Lydia, getting a carrot out of her pocket. Henry lifted his head but wasn't sufficiently tempted to give up his freedom for one measly carrot. He took a step farther away from them, toward the drive.

Lydia looked worried. "He can't go down the drive. He'd be over the gate in a second and then we'd never catch him."

"I'll cut him off," said James quickly. "If I go across

the grass, I can get to the gate and block him if he reaches it." He set off across the field. Mandy and Lydia edged toward Henry. Lydia waved the carrot again. Henry's nose twitched.

"Quietly now," Lydia murmured to Mandy, her eyes never leaving the goat. "While he's looking at me, see if you can get around in front of him and shoo him toward me, away from the drive."

Mandy started to sidle around the little goat. His ears twitched back and forth. She got a little bit closer and, all of a sudden, tripped over a cobblestone and crashed to the ground. Henry leaped up into the air and, turning on the spot, set off at a joyful canter down the drive.

Mandy scrambled to her feet and raced after him, her heart pounding. To her relief, she saw James running up the drive toward the goat, waving his arms. Henry snorted in surprise and then cantered back up the drive. He swerved past Mandy's outstretched arms.

"He's heading for the big field," gasped Mandy. "Come on, James!"

They raced up the drive. Suddenly, just as Henry reached the track that led toward the fields, there was a loud rattling. Henry stopped dead and bleated.

"Henry!" Lydia was standing by a shed, shaking the door vigorously. "Supper!"

Henry pricked his ears and set off toward Lydia at a

fast trot. Lydia opened the door and, as he pushed inside, she caught him firmly by his collar. "Got him!" she cried triumphantly.

Mandy and James looked at each other in amazement and hurried over. "What happened?" Mandy asked, astonished. "How did you get him to come?"

Lydia smiled and gave Henry his carrot. "This is my new granary. All the goats know that they get fed when they hear the door rattle. Henry's just too greedy to resist."

Mandy and James followed her as she led the little goat firmly back to the barn. The other goats were peering out of their pens, their ears pricked in excitement. "I'll have to give them a bit of food or they'll never settle down," said Lydia, putting Henry in his pen. "No more escaping for you," she told him firmly, as she fixed the safety clip securely onto the bolt on Henry's door.

"I'm sorry I left the barn door open," said James, shamefaced.

"All's well that ends well, as my father used to say," said Lydia. "I should have had the safety clip on, but when I'm cleaning out I often leave it off until I've finished going in and out."

Mandy and James helped Lydia scoop some oats and barley into buckets in her granary. The floor was flagged with large, gray stones. Around the walls stood strong metal feed bins, buckets, bags of old vegetables, and some huge, unopened sacks of oats and barley. Previously, Lydia had just kept the food in bins in the barn.

"I was offered a large amount of food at a cheap price," Lydia explained. "And I didn't have enough room in the barn so I decided that I would use this place." She threw the scoop back into the bin of barley. "The only trouble is, I hadn't bargained on the rats and mice." She nodded toward the feed bags. Several had holes nibbled in them and feed was spilling out onto the floor. "They're going to eat more of it than the goats if I don't do something soon."

"Can't you get some more feed bins?" asked James.

"They're very expensive," Lydia said. "And anyway it's not just in here that the mice are causing a problem. They're in the house and in the hayloft, too. They seem to be taking over the place. I've put down traps, but it doesn't seem to be stopping them."

"You should get a cat," said Mandy.

Lydia shook her head. "Me? No, I don't like cats. Cold, unfriendly creatures. Definitely not." She picked up the feed buckets. "Let's feed these goats and then we can get you that milk."

"Do you think Blossom will be scared of us today?" Mandy asked James as they walked through the Wards' yard gate. It was a question that had been preying on her mind. The night before, the little cat had been too ill to worry about their presence, but what would she be like now that she had recovered?

"There's only one way to find out," said James, pushing his glasses firmly onto his nose. They opened the shed door. Blossom was sitting up in the tub. She stared at them with her wide green eyes.

"Do you want some breakfast?" Mandy asked. She filled a bowl with the fresh goat's milk and placed it quietly by Blossom's tub. To her delight, the little cat jumped out of the tub, stalked over, and started to lap. Mandy cautiously knelt down beside her. Blossom continued to drink. Mandy stroked her. The tabby glanced up but her eyes had lost their fear. *She knows we helped her*, Mandy thought, a warm glow of happiness spreading through her.

"Look at the kittens," James said.

Mandy straightened up and looked in the tub. The three kittens were snuggled in a heap, their eyes tightly shut. Mandy knew that all kittens were born deaf and blind. She longed to touch them but thought Blossom might not like it. "I can't wait till they open their eyes," she said.

James nodded. "It happens when they are about five days old, doesn't it?" he asked.

"Well, sometime between three and ten days old," said Mandy. "We'll need to think of names for them. They should be called something that goes with Blossom."

James thought for a moment. "You can get different types of blossoms. There's cherry blossom, like on the tree outside. We could call one little girl kitten Cherry. And what about Peaches for the other one?"

"Cherry and Peaches," said Mandy, thinking about it. "Okay, they're good names." She pointed to the tabby one who looked just like Blossom. "That one can be Cherry and the other one can be Peaches." She frowned and looked at the ginger male kitten. "But what about him?"

James scratched his nose. "Apple? Apricot? Pear?"

"You can't call a cat any of those!" said Mandy, grinning.

They thought for a moment longer.

"What about William?" James suggested.

"But it's not a blossom," objected Mandy.

"It is," said James triumphantly. "You can get William pears, and William pear trees would have blossoms."

"Brilliant!" Mandy agreed, smiling. She looked at the little ginger kitten. "William it is, then."

Leaving Blossom to eat her breakfast, they knocked on the back door. Jane Ward answered. They told her about naming Blossom's kittens. "We've thought of names for Delilah's, too," she told them. "Do you want to come in and see them?"

"Where's Tara?" asked James, looking around as they walked through to the living room.

"Out with Bill on his rounds," Jane explained. "She keeps trying to get into the living room to see what's in there. But we're going to wait a few days before introducing her to the kittens."

"What names have you chosen?" Mandy asked eagerly as she and James followed Mrs. Ward to the living room.

"The two little girls are going to be Desdemona and Daisy and the two little boys are Daniel and Dylan."

Mandy and James knelt by the kittens' box. Delilah was awake and the kittens were feeding. The four little white bodies were all in a line.

"They look identical," said James. "How are you going to tell which is which?"

Jane smiled and pointed to four bottles of nail polish on the mantelpiece. Each bottle was a different color and each bottle had a kitten's name stuck to it. "I've put a dab of a different color on each kitten," she told them. "Just on one of their front claws. All I have to do is look at the color and then I know which kitten it is."

"That's clever," said Mandy. She peered closer. "So, which *is* which?"

"The bright pink is Desdemona, the pale pink is Daisy, the red is Dylan, and the plum color is Daniel."

The kittens squirmed and pushed to get at Delilah's milk. Mandy noticed one kitten seemed particularly good at edging the others out of the way. He scrabbled and shoved and climbed over his brother and sisters. Mandy checked the color of the nail polish. It was red. She checked the labels on the bottles. That meant he must be Dylan. She smiled. Using the nail polish was a really good way of telling the kittens apart.

"They don't do very much at the moment, do they?" said James, as one by one the kittens stopped drinking and fell asleep where they lay.

Jane shook her head. "They will when they start opening their eyes."

Mandy frowned. "Delilah has amber eyes but her mother, Duchess, has blue. Do you know what color eyes the kittens will have?"

"We hope amber," said Jane. "White cats with blue eyes are often deaf. Duchess isn't, but she's quite rare. All kittens have blue eyes to start with, but they start changing once the kittens reach three months old." She smiled rather anxiously at Mandy and James. "Fingers crossed, they'll all be fine."

Mandy looked down at the sleeping kittens, all snuggled into one big heap. They looked so perfect. She couldn't bear the thought that one or more of them might be deaf. Surely they would all be all right?

Mandy and James visited the two sets of kittens each day, calling in morning and evening when they stopped off to feed Blossom. "William's going exploring again," Mandy pointed out as she and James crouched by Blossom's tub after school on Tuesday.

Cherry and Peaches were lying contentedly beside their mother but William, the little ginger kitten, was slowly pushing himself across the bottom of the tub. He couldn't walk yet so he was sliding on his tummy, using his back legs. He reached the side of the tub and stopped.

James laughed. "I bet he's going to be adventurous when he gets older."

"Cherry's not." Mandy smiled, glancing at the little tabby kitten, who was snuggled as far as she could be into Blossom's soft fur. "She never leaves Blossom's side." She reached in and gently picked up Peaches. Blossom hardly flickered an eyelid. She was used to Mandy and James handling her precious kittens now. "What about you, Peaches?" Mandy said, feeling the tiny pinpricks of Peaches's claws. "What are you going to be like?"

The little tabby-and-white kitten lifted her head and blinked at her. "James!" Mandy gasped, almost dropping the kitten in amazement. "Look! She's opening her eyes!"

They gazed speechlessly at Peaches. She blinked again and this time kept her eyes open. She looked around. Her eyes were a deep, dark blue. Opening her mouth, she meowed.

Mandy and James laughed. Carefully, Mandy put her back into the tub. "That must mean that the others are about to open their eyes, too," she said. They picked up William and Cherry, but their eyes were still closed.

"Maybe they will have opened them by tomorrow," said James, hopefully.

James was right. When they stopped off to feed Blossom the next morning, they found William and Cherry blinking in the shaft of sunlight that was shining in through the dusty shed window. "They won't be able to see very much to start with," said Mandy. "But their eyesight will gradually get stronger." She smiled. "Don't they look adorable?"

Just then, there was the sound of feet coming along the path and Jane Ward poked her head around the shed door. She was wearing her dressing gown and slippers. "I thought I heard you come in through the gate."

She looked pleased and excited. "Come and see Delilah's kittens. They've just opened their eyes!"

Mandy and James peered into Delilah's box. Desdemona, Daisy, Dylan, and Daniel all blinked up, their large eyes looking extra blue against the white of their fur.

"It's amazing how Delilah's and Blossom's kittens have opened their eyes at exactly the same time," said Mandy.

Jane Ward nodded. "And now that they've opened their eyes, the fun and games will *really* start. They'll be trying to walk in another week."

"Seven kittens!" said James. "Just think what mischief they could get up to!"

It took a while for the kittens to get used to walking, but by the time they were almost three weeks old, they were all toddling around on their short, unsteady legs. Most of the time they moved around with their large heads close to the ground, stopping occasionally to roll over and play. Mandy felt that she could quite happily have sat and watched them all day.

"Each day they do something different," she told her mom as she helped clean up after Thursday evening clinic visits. "They've started trying to bite each other now. Dylan was the first to start and now they're all doing it." She squeezed out the mop she was using and looked across at her mother. "Mom . . ." She stopped.

Dr. Emily looked up from sorting her paperwork. "Is there something on your mind?" she asked, studying Mandy's face.

Mandy nodded. Ever since Mrs. Ward had mentioned the link between blue eyes and deafness she had been thinking about Delilah's kittens. "What would happen if one of Delilah's kittens was deaf?"

Dr. Emily rubbed her forehead. "Well, I expect Bill and Jane Ward would try to find a good home for it but it would be difficult." She saw Mandy's worried face. "How old are the kittens now?"

"Three weeks old tomorrow."

Dr. Emily smiled. "And adorable?"

"Completely," said Mandy.

Dr. Emily tidied up her paperwork. "If they're three weeks, then they should be about old enough to have their hearing tested."

Mandy's eyes lit up. "Is it difficult to test them? Could I do it?"

Dr. Emily shook her head. "Oh, no, you *definitely* need a trained vet." She looked thoughtful. "If Jane doesn't mind, I could stop in after morning clinic on Saturday. Maybe I'll give her a call and see what she thinks."

"Could you?" asked Mandy eagerly. If there was a way of telling whether any of the kittens were deaf, then she wanted to know. But what would happen if one of the kittens *was* deaf? What would the Wards do then?

The four white kittens walked unsteadily around their run, stopping occasionally to climb over one another. Dylan pawed at Daisy's face and knocked her over. She rolled on her back and he tried to bite her. Daniel watched from a safe distance. He was the most timid of Delilah's four kittens.

It was Saturday afternoon. Jane Ward had gladly accepted Dr. Emily's offer to come and test the kittens' hearing. Dr. Emily took the kittens out of the box one at a time and examined them thoroughly. Delilah sat on the carpet and watched. "Very healthy," Dr. Emily pronounced.

"But are they deaf?" Mandy asked anxiously. "How will you tell?"

Dr. Emily smiled. "Ah, yes. Now this is a really complicated test. Are you watching carefully?"

Mandy nodded. Dr. Emily put Dylan down on a towel on the floor. He took a few wobbly steps. Mandy waited eagerly. She wondered what her mother was going to do.

All of a sudden, Dr. Emily clapped her hands loudly, a

little way behind the kitten. Dylan started and looked around curiously.

"There we are," said Dr. Emily with a smile at Mandy. "Not deaf."

Mandy stared. "Is that all you do? But you said it was really complicated!"

Dr. Emily's green eyes twinkled. "I just wanted an excuse to see the kittens."

"Mom!"

Dr. Emily picked Dylan up and cuddled him. "I love kittens." She turned to Jane. "Don't worry, I won't be charging you for this visit." Putting Dylan in the box, she took Daniel out. "You have to be sure that the kitten can't see you doing it," she explained to Mandy. "And you can't clap too close or drop something on the floor to make a noise, because then the kitten might feel the vibrations and turn around."

Mandy watched as her mother tested Daniel. He, too, was given the "all clear," although he almost fell over in fright at the loud sound. "Scaredy-cat!" said Mandy, laughing and putting him back in the safety of the box. She turned to her mom. "Can I try with the next one?" When Dr. Emily nodded, Mandy carefully picked Desdemona out of the box and put her down on the floor. When Desdemona's back was turned, she clapped her hands.

Desdemona jumped. Mandy smiled in relief. "She's all right."

Daisy was the last kitten to be tested. Mandy held her breath and clapped. To her delight, Daisy jumped and looked around as well. Seeing Mandy, she came toward her, stopping and putting her tiny paws on Mandy's knee. Daisy meowed loudly, looking up with her dark blue eyes.

"I think she wants to be picked up," said Jane Ward with a laugh. "She seems to love being cuddled. She's always the first to come over when you look in the pen." Mandy scooped the little kitten up and cradled her in the crook of her arm.

Jane Ward and Dr. Emily stood up. "I think you've got a wonderful, healthy litter there," said Dr. Emily. "It's a pleasure to see kittens so well looked after."

"It's all really down to Delilah," said Jane. "She does most of the looking after, the cleaning, and feeding."

"Where is Delilah?" asked Mandy, putting Daisy back into the box and looking around.

Delilah was no longer in the living room. "She's probably gone for a little stroll," said Jane. "She's just started leaving the kittens for longer periods of time. I'm trying to keep an eye on her, though. I don't really think she's got her road sense back yet."

Mandy looked out of the window. Delilah was walking across the grass of the front yard. As Mandy watched, she jumped onto the gatepost. "Mrs. Ward," said Mandy, anxiously. "Delilah got out."

Jane looked out of the window and sighed. "I'd better go get her." She headed for the back door.

"And I'd better be getting back home," said Dr. Emily, picking up her bag and following Mrs. Ward out. "I take it you're going to stay here for a bit longer, Mandy?"

Before Mandy had a chance to reply, there was a screech of brakes from the road.

Mandy looked back at the gatepost. "Delilah!" she gasped. Delilah was no longer there. Mandy shot a horrified look at her mother. They raced down the path toward the road.

Five

"Oh, no!" cried Jane Ward, her hands flying to her mouth. Delilah was lying completely still in the middle of the road.

"Quick, Mandy!" said Dr. Emily. They ran over and knelt beside the motionless cat. A sob caught in Mandy's throat. Delilah's eyes were closed. Bright-red blood was spurting out of a wound in her leg.

"She's still breathing," said Dr. Emily. She looked up quickly. "We need to get her off this road. Can you find me something flat to move her on, Mandy? We need to keep her as still as possible."

"There's a piece of wood in the shed," said Mandy.

"Get that, please. Jane, can you keep an eye on the road and check that nothing else comes?" Not waiting for an answer, Dr. Emily bent her head and gently started to examine Delilah.

Mandy ran to the shed. Her heart was racing, her breath was coming in short gasps. Hot tears burned against the back of her eyes, but she knew she had to keep a clear head if she was going to help her mother try to save Delilah.

Together, they eased Delilah's still, white body onto the plank of wood and lifted her to the side of the road. Jane hovered anxiously behind them. "I can't believe the driver didn't even stop," she kept repeating dazedly.

Dr. Emily opened her bag and knelt beside Delilah. "She's in shock," she said to Mandy. "We need to stop this bleeding and get her to Animal Ark immediately." She pressed firmly on the blood vessel to stem the furious flow. "Can you pass me a thick wad of dressing and a bandage from my bag?"

Mandy already had the bag open. She held Delilah's leg steady while her mother applied a pressure bandage. Without needing to be asked, she passed over the tape and the scissors. Her heart was pounding but her mind was clear as she concentrated on assisting her mother as efficiently as possible. Every second was vital. "That will do," Dr. Emily said, throwing everything into her bag and jumping swiftly to her feet. "Let's get her into the Land Rover."

They lifted Delilah carefully into the back. "Will you be able to save her?" Jane Ward whispered. Mandy turned and saw the anguish on her face.

Dr. Emily reached to shut the back of the Land Rover. "I can't tell, Jane." Her green eyes were warm with sympathy. "But I promise we'll do all we can. Can you follow us to the clinic? We'll be able to find out more there."

It was silent and tense in the Land Rover on the way back to Animal Ark. Mandy felt sick to her stomach. "Mandy," Dr. Emily said, glancing over, "can you call the clinic and let them know we're coming in, please?"

Mandy punched the numbers into the cell phone.

"Animal Ark." It was her dad. Hearing his deep, warm voice, Mandy almost gave way to the tears that were burning behind her eyes, but she forced herself to speak calmly. She explained quickly about Delilah. "We're coming straight in," she told him. "Mrs. Ward's following us."

"I'll get the operating room ready," Dr. Adam said quickly. "Try not to worry. You'll be here soon."

But would "soon" be too late? thought Mandy. She put the phone down and turned to look at Delilah. Her heart sank. The cat was lying motionless in the back. *Oh, please*, she thought, a lump of tears swelling in her throat. *Please let us be in time.*

Dr. Adam and Simon were waiting at Animal Ark. They hurried out as the Land Rover stopped, and lifted Delilah out of the back. Dr. Emily grabbed her white coat from the office and followed them into the operating room.

"Can I come in?" asked Mandy, running after her.

Dr. Emily shook her head. "Not this time, Mandy," she said gently.

Mandy stared as the door of the operating room closed. She was normally allowed in to watch operations. Why not this one? The only answer possible thumped in her heart. Her mom thought Delilah wasn't going to survive.

The waiting-room door flew open and Jane Ward came hurrying in. "Where is she?" she asked wildly.

"In the operating room," said Mandy.

Jane sank down onto one of the seats and buried her head in her hands. Mandy could see her shoulders shaking. She sat down next to her. "Mom and Dad will do everything they can," she said, trying to sound as confident as possible. Jane didn't reply.

Bill Ward arrived. With tears running down her cheeks, Jane told him what had happened. He sat down beside her and took her hand.

The minutes ticked by slowly.

Half an hour later, the door opened. All three of them jumped to their feet as Dr. Emily came out. She was pushing the hair back from her face. Mandy searched her eyes. What news did she have?

"What's happened?" asked Jane. "Is she . . . ? Is she . . . ?"

"Delilah's badly injured but we think she's going to survive," said Dr. Emily.

Relief rushed through Mandy, her legs went wobbly, and she suddenly had to sit down again. Bill hugged Jane.

"The X rays show that Delilah has a slight fracture of her pelvis and two broken ribs," Dr. Emily continued. "But luckily there appears to be no internal hemorrhaging. The next twenty-four hours will be critical but at the moment the signs are good."

"Can we see her?" asked Jane.

"Of course, come through."

Dr. Adam and Simon were putting things away. They left the operating room so Dr. Emily could talk to the Wards. Mandy went straight to where Delilah was lying on the operating table. A new bandage had replaced the old one on the cat's leg. Her eyes were closed but her breathing had slowed down.

Bill came and stood behind Mandy. "Poor girl," he said, shaking his head.

Dr. Emily got out a set of X rays and displayed them against a light table. She pointed out the fracture in Delilah's pelvis. "Luckily, Delilah has escaped with only a slight fracture. Serious fractures in this area nearly always result in the cat needing to be put to sleep."

"Do you have to operate or anything to mend it?" asked Jane.

Dr. Emily shook her head. "Hopefully, this and the broken ribs will self-heal," she said. "It may take up to two months and she will have to have restricted movement for at least part of the time, in order to avoid any aggravation of her injuries." She switched off the light table and unclipped the X rays. "Because of the kittens, I think she should stay here at Animal Ark while she recovers."

"For how long?" Jane asked.

Dr. Emily stroked Delilah's head. "We'll have to see how her recovery goes. It may be three weeks, possibly more." She looked sympathetic. "You can come and see her as often as you want."

"I'll look after her," promised Mandy. "I'll make sure she's as happy as possible while she's here."

"Thanks, Mandy," said Mrs. Ward, but her face was troubled. "So what does this mean for the kittens?"

There was a pause. "There are three options," Dr. Emily said at last, tucking a strand of loose hair behind her left ear. "One, to find a cat who has lost her own kittens to act as a foster mother. Unfortunately I don't know of any such cats at the moment, and even if I did there's no guarantee that she would accept the kittens anyway. Two, you can hand-rear the kittens."

Jane nodded. "That's what I thought we'd have to do."

"They will need to be fed every three hours, starting at about six in the morning and going through till midnight. It will be an almost full-time job for the next three or four weeks until they are weaned. Luckily, they are old enough to go through the night without being fed."

Jane started to look worried. "But I'm at work all day and Bill's not in until after one-thirty." She frowned. "We could maybe ask someone to help us."

Bill scratched his chin. "It's asking a lot of anyone. Who do we know who could spare the time?"

Mandy looked at her mom. "Couldn't the kittens come and stay here?"

Dr. Emily shook her head. "With the lambing season coming to its peak we're just too busy, Mandy. Simon will have enough to do, coping with the patients here while Dad and I are out on call."

"You said there was a third option?" said Bill.

Dr. Emily sighed. "The third option is to put them to sleep."

"No!" gasped Mandy, horrified.

Jane immediately started shaking her head. "Oh, no! No, I couldn't."

"Mom, that's . . ."

Dr. Emily shot Mandy a very stern look and Mandy swallowed her words. She knew that, no matter how hard it was, she must never interfere when her mother was giving a professional opinion. Deep down, her mom would no sooner want to have the kittens put to sleep than Mandy herself, but, as a vet, it was her duty to give her clients what she felt to be the most honest and practical advice possible.

Dr. Emily's eyes searched the Wards' faces.

"Oh, what are we going to do?" Jane said despairingly.

"Mandy, would you go and get a cage ready for Delilah in the residential unit, please," Dr. Emily said. Mandy stared desperately at her. She couldn't bear the thought that the kittens' fate would be decided without her in the room.

"Mandy," Dr. Emily insisted, her eyes demanding obedience.

Not trusting herself to speak, Mandy turned and walked out of the room.

As soon as she shut the door, a huge sob burst from her. She ran into the residential unit and collapsed in a heap by the door, giving way to a flood of tears. Surely the Wards wouldn't put Delilah's kittens to sleep? How could they? If only there was something she could do. She thought of how the kittens had been earlier that day, play-fighting and toddling around their box. But it was the Wards' decision. Burying her head in her hands, she cried noisily.

The door opened. "Mandy?" It was Dr. Adam. His face creased in concern. "Mandy, whatever's the matter?"

"Oh, Dad!" sobbed Mandy, hardly able to get the words out. "It's the kittens!"

Dr. Adam hurried over and, kneeling down beside her, put his arm around her slim shoulders. "Come on, tell me all about it."

Her body shaking with great gasping sobs, Mandy explained. "There's no one to look after them," she said. "The Wards are out at work and they don't know anyone who can help. They're going to be put to sleep! Oh, Dad, I can't bear it!"

"Hang on, hang on," said Dr. Adam, his kind eyes probing her face. "Aren't you and James on vacation next week?"

Mandy nodded as she sobbed against his shoulder. Suddenly, the significance of his words hit her. She sat bolt upright and stared at him. "You mean James and I could help look after them?"

Dr. Adam nodded.

"But we're only off for a week," Mandy said despairingly. "And the kittens will need hand-rearing for at least three or four more weeks."

"But a week gives you time to try and find someone else who can take over when you go back to school," pointed out Dr. Adam. "Isn't it worth a try?" He squeezed her shoulder. "Look, why don't you go and ask Mom?"

Mandy stared at him, the tears drying on her face. "Do you think she'll say yes?"

"What do you think?" said Dr. Adam.

Dr. Emily and the Wards looked up in surprise as Mandy burst into the operating room. "We can help you!" she cried. "James and I! We're off next week. We can look after the kittens while you're at work." She babbled out the words as fast as she could.

For a moment they all just stared.

"But, Mandy, love, what will happen when you and James go back to school at the end of the week?" asked Dr. Emily, the quickest to recover.

"We'll think of *something*," said Mandy desperately. "We can ask around. We'll find someone who can help." She looked around at them all. Her blue eyes started to plead. "At least give us a chance to try."

Dr. Emily turned to the Wards. "Well, it's up to you."

Jane Ward's face broke into a smile. "We'd really love your help, Mandy, wouldn't we, Bill?"

"If you're sure you've got the time?" he said to Mandy.

Mandy nodded eagerly. She looked at her mother and saw the relief in her eyes. "Well, it certainly does seem like a good solution," Dr. Emily said. She shot Mandy a glance. "It will be hard work, though. Sometimes kittens don't like formula milk."

"I don't care how hard I've got to work," said Mandy, her own eyes shining with determination. "I just want Delilah's kittens to have a chance."

Six

"Do you have everything we need?" James called as they biked along. As soon as Mandy had called him to tell him about how they were going to spend their time off he had come around quickly.

Mandy nodded. They were on their way to give the kittens their first bottle feed. Her backpack was heavy with feeding bottles, bags of formula milk, and other equipment that her mother had thought they might need.

Jane Ward was waiting for them in the kitchen. She had emptied a shelf in one of the cupboards for them. "You can leave everything in here. Out, Tara!" she said, as the dog tried to investigate the bags of formula milk. "I think you'd better go outside." Taking Tara firmly by the collar, she steered her out into the backyard.

Mandy opened a bag of the milk. "Do you have a fork we could use, Mrs. Ward?"

Jane handed her a fork and watched as James measured out the fine, creamy-colored powder with a tiny scoop, and then Mandy used the fork to mix the powder with some water. "You look like you've done this before," she said.

Mandy grinned. "We have. Lots of times."

"Kittens, puppies, lambs, goats," James put in. "We've helped bottle-feed all sorts of young animals."

Jane smiled and went to fetch the first two kittens. "So, I'm getting a lesson from the experts, then."

After ten minutes of trying to get Dylan and Daniel to accept some milk, Mandy and James were feeling far from expert. The milk was on their hands, on their jeans, and on the kittens' fur, but none of it had seemed to go into a kitten's mouth. "I see what Mom meant about kittens sometimes being awkward!" said Mandy, struggling to hold Dylan. "Come on, you *want* this milk."

But Dylan was adamant that he didn't. He shut his mouth tight and moved his head around.

On the other side of the table, James was faring as

badly with Daniel. "This is a nightmare!" he said to Mandy, as Daniel almost managed to throw himself onto the floor.

"They don't seem to want to drink anything," said Jane, looking worried.

The two little kittens meowed pitifully.

Blossom poked her head around the kitchen door. She stalked over to James and stared at him.

"It's all right, Blossom," James said. "We're not hurting them."

"We're not managing to feed them much, either," said Mandy.

"Should I hold one?" Jane offered. She took Daniel and held him firmly. It was a bit easier with two people — one to hold and one to feed, and at last both kittens had taken some milk. Mandy cleaned them up with a warm, damp cloth and then put them back in the box.

"Time for the next two," she said to James. Looking less than enthusiastic, James picked up Daisy. "I hope she's not as bad as Daniel," he said.

If anything, Daisy was even worse. By the time Daisy and Desdemona were fed, both Mandy and James were once again covered in spilled milk. "Thank goodness that's over!" said James, putting Daisy down in the box.

Mandy watched the kittens. Normally, after eating,

they would fall asleep, curled up by Delilah, but now they wandered around, opening their mouths wide and meowing. She sighed. They were missing their mom.

"If only there was something we could do to make them happier," she said. But she knew the only thing that would make a difference would be Delilah.

James and Mandy agreed to meet the following morning at eight o'clock to feed Blossom and to help the Wards with the kittens' nine o'clock feed. As soon as Mandy got back to Animal Ark, she went straight to the residential unit to check on Delilah. It was Simon's afternoon off, but he had offered to stay to keep an eye on Delilah's recovery. He was sitting next to her cage, reading a book about badgers. "Hi, there," he said as Mandy came in.

"How is she?" Mandy asked eagerly, looking in the cage. Delilah was lying flat out on a fleecy white blanket. Her breathing was slow and deep. Her eyes were closed.

"She's coming around slowly," Simon said, standing up and looking over Mandy's shoulder. "But she'll be kept sedated so she doesn't try to move too much at the moment. How were the kittens?"

Mandy sighed. "Oh, Simon, it's so difficult to get them

to feed." She looked at him hopefully; he could usually be relied on when it came to looking after animals. "Any ideas?"

But this time even Simon couldn't help her. "Sorry," he said, shrugging sympathetically. "But I don't think there are any magic solutions to bottle-feeding kittens. Just keep trying. I've got a book on cats with a good chapter on bringing up orphan kittens — if you want to read it."

"Yes, please!" said Mandy. "I think I need all the advice I can get."

Simon looked at her. "You know, it's not going to be easy looking after four kittens."

"Why does everyone keep telling me that?" Mandy exclaimed. "I don't *care* how hard it is as long as Delilah's kittens are all right!"

The next morning Mandy summoned all her determination. They would get the kittens to drink the milk. She wondered how the Wards had got on with the feeding since she and James had left the evening before.

One look at Jane Ward's strained face told her all she needed to know. "They just don't seem to want to drink," Jane said as she let them in the following morning. "We've only managed to get a tiny bit down them and they just keep crying all the time. I tried putting a hot-water bottle in with them but it made no difference." She sighed.

Just then Bill came back from walking Tara. "Maybe we'll have more luck with all four of us," he suggested, as Tara enthusiastically said hello to Mandy and James.

They managed to get the kittens to take a little bit of the milk but it was hard work. "Will you be all right to-morrow morning on your own?" Jane asked.

Mandy saw the worry in her eyes and smiled confidently. "I'm sure we'll be fine," she said.

When they arrived the next morning, they could hear the kittens meowing inside the house. "Let's hope they're hungry this morning," James said.

Bill had taken Tara on his rounds to keep her out of Mandy and James's way. "If you get one of the kittens, I'll get the stuff out," Mandy said, opening the cupboard in the kitchen.

"Which one shall we start with?" James asked.

Mandy considered. "Daisy," she decided. "At least she likes being picked up."

James went to the living room while Mandy got the bottles ready. She carefully scooped the formula milk powder out of the bag. It was important to get the measurements just right. She was concentrating hard when she heard James shouting her name. He sounded very agitated.

Mandy looked up in surprise as James came running back into the kitchen. "Mandy!" he gasped in alarm. "One of the kittens is gone!"

Mandy stared at him and then ran into the living room. Three little white faces looked up at her. By checking the color of the nail polish on the remaining kittens' claws, they worked out that Dylan was missing.

"He must have climbed out of the box," said James.

"But where has he gone?" said Mandy, looking around the room.

James started to look under chairs and behind the sofa. "He's got to be here somewhere," he said. "Help me look!"

Together, they moved every piece of furniture in the room but there was no sign of Dylan. They looked in the kitchen. They looked in the hall. They turned the living room upside down.

Mandy's heart was beating fast. "Where is he?"

"Could he have gotten outside?" asked James.

Mandy shook her head. "He's much too small to push the cat flap open."

James frowned. "Well, then, he's *got* to be in here somewhere. Kittens don't just disappear." He went through to the kitchen and looked around to see where a kitten might hide. He looked under the table and around the back of the stove. Mandy opened all the cupboards and even the fridge but there was no sign of Dylan.

"We've got to think logically," said James. "Where would a kitten hide?"

Just then, Blossom appeared and started weaving around Mandy's legs. "I'd better feed her," Mandy said, looking down.

"I'll keep looking for Dylan," said James. "I'm going to check upstairs. Maybe one of the Wards left the living room door open for a while."

Mandy mashed Blossom's meat up in her food bowl and poured out some goat's milk from the fridge. *Where was Dylan?* James had said they had to be logical, but they'd already covered all the obvious options.

Blossom meowed.

"Back in a minute," Mandy called to James. She hurried out of the door but Blossom seemed strangely reluctant to follow her. "It's your breakfast, come on," said Mandy. The little cat followed Mandy out, but kept looking back toward the house.

"Here we are," said Mandy, pushing open the door of the shed and putting the bowls down. Blossom settled down to eat. Mandy glanced quickly into the tub. The kittens were lying in a pile — ginger, tabby . . . Mandy frowned. There, in the center of the pile, was a fluffy white ear and a fluffy white tail. Her eyes widened. It was Dylan!

Blossom hadn't seemed to have noticed the extra kitten in her nest. Mandy quickly scooped Dylan out. The little white kitten nestled warmly in her arms, his blue eyes half shut, his tail twitching just slightly. Mandy hurried back into the house with the precious bundle in her arms. "James! I found him!" she cried as she burst through the back door.

James came running down the stairs. He couldn't believe his eyes. "Where was he?"

"In the tub with Blossom's kittens."

"But how did he get there?" asked James, astonished.

Mandy hadn't a clue. "I'm just glad Blossom didn't notice him in with her kittens," she said. "Mother cats can be very protective of their litters." She kissed Dylan's fluffy white head. "The most important thing is that he's back now. He must be ready for his breakfast."

But Dylan was even less cooperative than usual. Mandy held him on her knee while James tried to give him the bottle, but Dylan scrunched up his face and flatly refused to open his mouth. The milk got into his eyes and ran down onto Mandy's arm. "We'll have to try later," said Mandy at last. "He's just not going to drink at the moment."

She put Dylan back in the pen. James picked up Desdemona. To their relief, Desdemona and then Daisy and Daniel did drink some of their milk. Dylan, meanwhile, simply curled up in a corner of the pen and went to sleep.

"You don't think he's ill, do you?" James asked when they had finished feeding the other three kittens, and had put them down to have a run around the living room.

Mandy picked Dylan up, but his breathing and heart rate seemed normal and his gums looked healthy and pink. He didn't seem to be in any distress so Mandy put him back in his corner. "I think he's okay," she said cautiously. "Maybe he'll have some milk later."

The sun was shining and Mandy and James went outside. They opened the door to Blossom's shed to let in some sunshine. Blossom's kittens were playing in the tub, patting at each other's faces, and climbing on top of each other.

William put his paws up against the side of the tub and meowed, his mouth opening to reveal a pink tongue and needle-sharp white teeth. "He wants to explore," said Mandy. She looked at James. "We could take them into the yard. They could play on the grass."

"But they haven't had any vaccinations yet," said James.

"They'll be fine in the yard," said Mandy. "They just shouldn't come into contact with any other cats." Blossom followed at their feet as they carried the three kittens into the yard. She sniffed each of the kittens when Mandy and James put them on the ground, and then lay down a little way off.

The three kittens looked hard at the grass. After staring at it and then sniffing it, they took a few cautious steps. Soon Cherry set off to explore a heap of blossoms. She rolled over, kicking her tiny legs in the air.

A piece of blossom fluttered toward Peaches. She watched it for a long moment and then clumsily tried to pounce on it. William came to join her, and together they patted at it and pounced again, landing in a tangle of legs and tails. Peaches lay down and tried to chew the blossom. Losing interest, William looked around and set off across the grass.

"How far do you think he will go?" James asked.

Mandy wasn't sure. Just as William got a short distance away, a car tooted its horn on the road. Terrified, William jumped in the air and scrambled back to the safety of the other kittens. He peered out nervously from behind Cherry, his ears pricked, his eyes wide.

"Poor William," laughed Mandy. "I hope that hasn't put him off exploring." But it obviously hadn't. A few minutes later, William set off again, eager as ever to explore.

Mandy remembered what she had been reading in Simon's book. "Soon Blossom will start teaching them to hunt," she said. "Kittens practice pouncing and stalking and leaping by playing with each other and with their mother. We'll have to bring Delilah's kittens out and bring them up just as Delilah would have done." The ideas bubbled out of her. "It will be really good. We can set up hunting games for them and bring all sorts of different foods and make them toys . . ."

"Hang on, Mandy!" James broke in. "First, we've got to find someone who can feed them when we go back to school next week."

The wind rushed out of Mandy's sails. She had been so busy thinking about how much fun it would be to bring up the kittens that she had forgotten all about going back to school next week. She had promised the Wards that they would find someone to help.

"They're still going to need feeding every three hours for at least another two weeks," James pointed out. "And the Wards have said they can't do it. We've got to think of something, otherwise . . ." His voice trailed off.

"We'll think of something," said Mandy, her eyes flashing with determination.

Seven

The following morning, Mandy and James unlocked the Wards' back door. Neither of them had thought of anyone who might be able to help with the kittens, although both had been thinking hard. "There has to be someone," Mandy said as she pushed the door open. "If only Grandma and Grandad weren't away."

"If only the kittens were easier to feed," said James as he followed her into the living room. "Then it might not be so difficult. But as it is . . ."

"James!" said Mandy, stopping dead. "Look!"

James's mouth dropped open. There were only two kittens. This time, Mandy didn't need to check the claws to see which kittens were still there. One of the kittens was sitting quietly at the back of the box, and the other was standing up against the side, asking to be picked up. "Dylan and Desdemona are missing," she said in dismay.

"But where have they gone?" James exclaimed.

Mandy looked quickly around. There was no sign of the missing kittens anywhere in the living room.

James hurried to the kitchen and scanned the room. "They're not here." He turned to Mandy. "You don't think they're going to be in Blossom's shed again, do you?"

Mandy stared at him. "There's only one way to find out!"

They hurried down the path to the shed and looked into the tub. There were five kittens inside.

"Quick, James!" said Mandy in alarm. "We've got to get Dylan and Desdemona out before Blossom notices."

They scooped the two Persian kittens out of the tub just as Blossom trotted in through the shed door.

Dylan and Daisy started to meow. "Shush, shush," Mandy said. Blossom stopped dead and looked up at the two white bundles in Mandy's and James's arms. Standing up on her hind legs she balanced against Mandy's leg. "It's all right, Blossom," Mandy said hastily. "Don't worry. We're taking them away."

Blossom trotted after them as they carried the kittens back into the house. She lingered outside the back door.

"That was close," said James. He frowned as he put Dylan back in the box. "I just don't understand *how* they are getting out." He examined the box. "The sides are just too high."

Mandy imagined what might have happened if Blossom had found the two white kittens in her tub. "We can't have them escaping like this. Anything could happen."

"We've got to find out how they're getting out, then," said James. "And stop them." He pushed his glasses up on his nose. "Let's hide and see what they do."

They went outside and peered in through the living room window. Delilah's kittens meowed loudly but nothing else happened. The minutes ticked by.

"It's a bit cold out here," said Mandy, shivering and rubbing her arms. Suddenly, Blossom entered the living room. "We'd better stop her," said Mandy, alarmed. "We don't want her to go near Delilah's kittens."

With one quick spring, Blossom leaped into the box. "James! Quick!" gasped Mandy. "She'll hurt them!"

Mandy and James dashed around to the living room just as Blossom was leaping out of the pen with a kitten hanging in her mouth.

"What's she doing?" James gasped. He was about to grab Blossom when Mandy suddenly stopped him.

"Wait! It's all right!" she said. "She's just carrying it. Watch!"

They stood like statues as Blossom walked past them with little Dylan swinging from her mouth. She padded across the carpet, into the kitchen, and out the open door. They followed at a safe distance and saw her enter the shed. They opened the door a crack and watched as she gently put Dylan into the tub.

"So *that's* how they got there," Mandy said softly. Blossom looked at her and James with an unblinking green stare.

"But why?" asked James.

Mandy didn't have an answer. "Let's see what she does next," she whispered.

They moved back into the yard and, from the safe distance of the cherry blossom tree, watched as Blossom returned into the house. And reappeared with Daisy in her mouth and took her to the shed, too. Back she went, and when she came out, she was carrying Desdemona. But this time when she went into the shed, she did not come out again.

"She's left Daniel in the house," said Mandy, astonished.

Mandy and James crept up to the door and eased it

open. Blossom was lying on her side feeding Delilah's three kittens along with her own.

"She's looking after them as if she was their mother," said James.

"But what about Daniel?" said Mandy.

They went back into the house. Little Daniel was standing all by himself. He was meowing loudly. Mandy scooped him up. "I don't know what's going on," she said, mystified. "I'm going to call Dad."

Jean answered the phone and put Mandy on to her father. "I'll come around," he said. "I've got an appointment over near Walton in half an hour. I can stop in on the way."

Ten minutes later, he arrived. Mandy and James took him to the shed where Blossom was feeding the kittens. All six were drinking hungrily. Dr. Adam smiled. "Well, well, well," he said. "It looks as though Blossom has decided to foster them. Has she been showing much interest in them?"

"Yes. Lots," said Mandy, rather shamefaced. "I thought she might be trying to harm them and kept her away."

"You were right to be cautious," Dr. Adam reassured her. "But it sounds like she was just worried about them. It's excellent news for the Wards."

Mandy looked at him. "So she'll be their foster

mother for good? I mean, not just today but until Delilah comes back?"

Dr. Adam nodded. "The most important step is over. She's accepted them, even welcomed them, I'd say. Now she'll bring them up as her own."

Mandy thought about the one little kitten who was still in the box. "But what about Daniel?"

Dr. Adam rubbed his beard. "I think Blossom is trying to increase her feeding load little by little; taking one kitten, then two, and now three. Hopefully, she will take him on as well." He smiled. "With all these kittens to feed she's going to need extra food herself. Keep up with the goat's milk, too. It's excellent for mothers who are feeding, and kittens as well when they get a bit older."

"We've almost run out," James said, looking at Mandy. "We'd better go and get some more."

"But what about Daniel?" asked Mandy. She couldn't bear to leave the tiny kitten crying by himself in the empty box.

"I'll go," said James. "You stay here."

Mandy waved good-bye to her dad and James and then returned to the living room. Daniel was meowing piteously. Mandy picked him up and, taking him to the kitchen, made up some formula milk. He was obviously hungry. He accepted quite a bit of the milk before starting to shake his head and struggle. Mandy put down the bottle. He cuddled into the crook of her arm. Looking down at the tiny, vulnerable creature, she felt her heart twist. It was so sad seeing him all on his own.

The sound of the cat flap made her look up. Blossom came into the kitchen and headed for the living room. "Blossom!" Mandy called.

Blossom stopped and looked around. She saw the kitten on Mandy's knee and trotted over. Hardly daring to breathe, Mandy gently placed Daniel on the floor.

Blossom stared up at Mandy. "Please take him," Mandy whispered, looking into Blossom's wide green eyes. The cat looked down at the kitten and then, picking him up by the scruff of his neck, turned and trotted toward the door. Mandy's heart leaped. She hurried to the door, watching in delight as Blossom carried Daniel down the path to the shed.

This, Mandy thought, *really is the perfect way to spend a Saturday afternoon*. She and James sat on the grass in the Wards' front yard, watching the kittens play in the sunshine. Bill Ward was standing by the cherry tree. "I still can't believe she took them all on," he said, looking at Blossom. The little tabby cat was standing on all fours on Mandy's lap, rubbing her head affectionately against Mandy's shoulder.

Mandy tickled her under the chin. "You're a very special cat, aren't you, Blossom?" she said. She ran a hand down the cat's shiny coat, pleased to find that her fingers no longer bumped painfully over every rib. The kittens were now four weeks old and getting livelier by the day.

"Dylan!" said James as the kitten bounced sideways up to Desdemona and knocked her over. Peaches hurried over and tried to pounce on their waving tails. She was always trying to catch things. Mandy was sure that she was going to be the first to learn to stalk and pounce properly.

There was a sudden crash from inside the shed. "What's that?" said Jane Ward in alarm.

Mandy did a quick kitten count. "Oh, no, William's missing!" She jumped to her feet and hurried to the shed. A large box lay upturned on the floor inside. Packets of seeds and gardening gloves were scattered everywhere.

Mandy lifted the box up. "William!" she exclaimed. The little ginger kitten looked up in surprise and then started to investigate the seeds on the floor.

"He must have pulled it off," said James, pointing to a strip of fabric that hung from the box. "I bet he tried to claw at that."

"Don't let him get to those seeds," said Bill Ward suddenly. "They'll be poisonous if he eats one."

Mandy whisked the kitten off the floor. "What are we going to do with you?" she scolded him.

Bill scratched his head. "I should really get this shed cleaned up," he said. "There's all sorts of things in here that aren't safe, and soon the kittens are going to be able to get out of that tub by themselves."

"We'll help," offered Mandy.

It took most of the afternoon to sort out the shed. By the end of it, the Wards' spare bedroom was covered with plastic sheeting and filled with garden equipment. Forks and spades leaned against the clothes closet. The dressing table was covered with cardboard boxes containing packets of seeds, weedkillers, and plant food. Pots littered the floor. "It'll never be the same again!" Jane said, but then she laughed. "At least the kittens will be safe."

Back in the shed, Bill leaned a plank against the tub so the kittens could get in and out easily. "They can explore in here as much as they like now," he said. "We can shut the door if we want to keep them in, or open it to let them into the yard."

Mandy changed the newspaper in the tub. "Perfect!" she said.

Jane picked up little Daisy, who was trying to climb up her leg. "It's going to be so hard when it comes to letting them all go."

"Have you got homes for them?" Mandy asked.

"We've had lots of inquiries," Jane told her. "We're going to keep one ourselves. In another two weeks or so we'll let people come to see them."

"Which one are you going to keep?" James asked.

Jane Ward looked around at Delilah's kittens and shook her head. "I don't know. It's impossible to decide." She looked at the little kitten in her arms. "Maybe Daisy."

As Mandy and James started off for home there was a question in Mandy's mind. "Mrs. Ward's got people who want Delilah's kittens," she said. "But what are we going to do about Blossom's?"

"I guess we'd better start looking for homes for them," said James.

"It won't be easy," said Mandy with a frown, remembering other times when they had tried to find homes for litters of kittens.

"It's going to be even harder to find a home for Blossom," James pointed out. "We haven't heard anything from the notices we put up. It really does look as if she was abandoned."

Mandy's heart sank. James was right. If it was difficult enough finding homes for cute kittens, it was bound to be twice as difficult finding a home for an adult cat.

Her mind was still on the problem when she sat down for supper that night. Dr. Adam had cooked a huge dish of macaroni and cheese. He brought it out of the oven, placed it in the center of the table, and picked up an enormous serving spoon.

"I'll serve," said Dr. Emily quickly.

"It smells delicious, Dad," said Mandy.

"I suppose I can always have seconds," said Dr. Adam, looking ruefully at the small portion Dr. Emily had put on his plate.

Mandy grinned. "Not if you want to be able to fit into those jeans much longer!"

She picked up her fork and started to tell them about looking for homes for Blossom's kittens.

"You could try advertising," suggested Dr. Adam. "Put up a notice at school maybe? And one in the clinic?"

"There are already so many kittens advertised," said Mandy, thinking of the clinic bulletin board. It had two kitten ads up already.

"Well, I'll keep my ears open," promised Dr. Adam. "I suppose a more difficult task is going to be finding a home for Blossom."

Mandy nodded and then looked hopefully at her parents. "Mom . . ."

"No," said Dr. Emily, recognizing the look. "Don't even think about asking. You know the rule, Mandy. We can't keep unwanted animals. We'd be overrun."

Mandy sighed. It was the one rule that her parents were both very strict about. "Maybe the Wards will keep her," she said. "I'll ask."

Dr. Emily frowned. "I thought they were planning to keep one of Delilah's kittens?"

Mandy nodded.

"Then I'm sure they won't want another cat. Ask them if you want, but don't be too disappointed if the answer's no." Just then the phone rang. "I'll get it," Dr. Emily said, jumping up. She was on call that night.

"Animal Ark. Dr. Emily speaking."

Mandy and her father listened. Was it a work call? Another lambing?

"Right . . . Okay . . . I see . . . How much? . . . Okay, don't worry, I'll be around as soon as I can." Dr. Emily put down the phone and hurried back to the table. She was already tying back her long hair. "That was Lydia Fawcett," she said, picking up her sweater from the chair. "One of her goats is ill."

"Which one? What's the matter?" asked Mandy anxiously.

"Henry, one of her youngsters. He's eaten some rat poison."

"Oh, no!" gasped Mandy.

"I said I'd go up there right away."

"Can I come?" asked Mandy, jumping up. Dr. Emily nodded.

"Good luck," called Dr. Adam as they hurried out of the door.

Eight

It was getting dark by the time Mandy and Dr. Emily reached High Cross Farm. A light shone from the barn. "Quick, Mandy!" said Dr. Emily, setting off across the cobbles. Mandy ran after her, her heart thumping. When they opened the barn door they found Lydia sitting in Henry's pen. The little goat's head was hanging down near the straw, his sides heaving in and out, his eyes half closed.

"He's been like this for the last half hour," said Lydia, looking up at them with worried eyes.

"Okay. I need to see the carton the poison came in," said Dr. Emily, taking charge. "Have you got it, Lydia?"

"It's in the kitchen." Lydia hurried to get it while Dr. Emily checked Henry's heart rate and breathing.

Mandy crouched down beside the goat's head. She rubbed his ears but his eyes hardly even flickered in her direction. He bleated unhappily. "Will he be all right, Mom?"

"It depends on what poison it was that Lydia used," said Dr. Emily. "Ah, here she is."

Lydia reappeared with a large plastic tub. She handed it to Dr. Emily. "I've never bought rat poison before," she said, and Mandy could see from her eyes how upset she was. "I bought it this morning and put it down in the granary." She ran a hand through her hair, making it stand up at all angles. "Henry let himself out. I found him in there and it was nearly all gone. That, and about half a sack of barley."

Dr. Emily was inspecting the back of the tub. "It's okay," she said quickly. "It's a warfarin-based poison. Warfarin stops the blood from clotting. It's fatal for rats and mice but doesn't affect goats in nearly the same way. Their digestive system is far stronger. What we need to do is to give him an injection of vitamin K." She took a syringe out of her bag and started to fill it with a clear liquid.

"So he'll get better?" asked Mandy.

Dr. Emily nodded as she injected the vitamin into

Henry's neck and patted him. "I would say he'll be right as rain in twenty-four hours."

"But he looks so miserable," said Mandy, looking at the sad little goat with his lowered head and half-shut eyes. As if to prove her right, Henry bleated sorrowfully again.

Dr. Emily smiled. "I think we'll find that that's just a rather nasty stomachache from having eaten so much barley. I'll give him something to help that as well, but I don't think a stomachache is going to threaten his life."

Lydia looked rather embarrassed. "Well," she said, coughing. "I'm sorry I called you out, Dr. Emily. But I did think it was serious. I won't take up any more of your time."

"Don't worry," said Dr. Emily. "He needed the vitamin K injection anyway." She smiled at Lydia. "The most important thing is that he is going to be all right. Now, how about a cup of tea?"

"My pleasure," said Lydia.

Mandy and her mother followed Lydia down to the farmhouse and into the old-fashioned kitchen. Great, dark, oak beams supported the ceiling. Books littered every surface. Mandy had to move some off a chair to be able to sit down.

Lydia filled a whistling kettle at the shallow sink by the window and put it on the old range to boil.

"So, what happened?" Dr. Emily asked curiously. "How *did* Henry get to the poison?"

Lydia brought over three chipped cups and saucers and sat down. "It was my fault really. He was in his pen with the safety bolt on." She sighed. "I went to catch Houdini and didn't bolt the barn door. By the time I got back with Houdini, the barn door was open, the granary door was open, and Henry had eaten most of the bait on the granary floor, as well as the sack of barley next to it."

"But how did he get out of his pen if you had left the safety bolt on?" asked Mandy.

"He must have worked out how to open it with his teeth," said Lydia. "I've always known he was a clever one. I'm just going to have to fix a bottom bolt onto his pen door. That should keep him in."

"So, what are you going to do about the rats and mice?" Dr. Emily asked as Lydia poured out the tea.

"Not put rat bait down, that's for sure. It's far too risky with goats like Henry and Houdini around." Lydia shrugged. "I just don't know."

Dr. Emily glanced quickly at Mandy. "You'll just have to get a cat, Lydia."

Mandy stared. She remembered how adamant Lydia had been when she had made the same suggestion a few weeks ago. But perhaps now, after all that had just happened, she might change her mind. "You should, Lydia," she urged. "You could have one of Blossom's." She thought of the large farm and her eyes shone. "In fact, you could have all three of them!"

Lydia looked rather taken aback. "Well, you know how I feel about cats, Mandy. I just don't like them."

"But it's the perfect solution!" Mandy said, the words tumbling eagerly out of her mouth as she tried to convince her old friend. "How else are you going to keep the rats and mice away? You said they ignored the traps and you can't put poison down again."

"Well, maybe," Lydia said doubtfully.

"And Blossom's kittens are not at all cold and unfriendly," Mandy said, remembering what Lydia had said about cats. "They're cuddly and adorable and love people."

"Why don't you go and have a look at the kittens and see what you think?" suggested Dr. Emily.

"Then they could all have a home together!" said Mandy.

Lydia quickly shook her head. "I certainly wouldn't want more than two."

Mandy's face fell but then she brightened. At least two of the kittens would have a good home, and it might not be so bad finding a home for just one little kitten. "Come and see them," she pleaded. "You'll love them."

By the time Mandy and her mother left, Lydia had agreed to come and see the kittens the following weekend. "They'll be five weeks old by then," said Mandy.

"And when would they be ready to go to their new homes?" Lydia asked cautiously. "Not that I'm promising anything, you realize."

"From about eight weeks old," said Dr. Emily.

Lydia nodded rather halfheartedly. "Well, I'll come and see but, as I said, I'm absolutely not promising."

The following Saturday, James and Mandy arrived early at the Wards' house. They were determined to make the kittens look as beautiful as possible before Lydia came.

"Surely when she sees them, she won't be able to choose two and leave just one without a home," said Mandy.

They put Delilah's kittens out in the yard and then checked William, Peaches, and Cherry over carefully. All three kittens had soft, shiny coats and bright eyes. Blossom watched as Mandy and James inspected them for fleas.

"Not a thing," said James. He put down Cherry and she trotted off to play with William. Peaches joined them and together they chased a blossom blowing across the grass beneath the tree. Mandy noticed that they had stopped falling over as much when they pounced. Sometimes Peaches could even manage a running jump and a spring.

"Look at William!" said Mandy. William had discovered a snail and was licking it. Whenever any of the kittens encountered something new, they immediately tried to taste it. Mandy was very relieved that they had cleared out the shed so thoroughly. It would be awful if the kittens tried to lick anything that was poisonous.

Blossom walked over to James and rubbed her head affectionately against his leg; then, sitting up on her back legs, she begged for attention. "I still can't believe she's a stray," said Mandy, bending down to stroke her. "She's so friendly now."

William and Desdemona came trotting over. They tried to pounce on Blossom's tail. She shook them off and stalked away.

"She's just starting to get fed up with them," said Mandy. "She'll stop letting them nurse in a week or two."

James watched as the two kittens charged after Blossom and jumped on her tail again, clawing at it, and chewing it with their needle-sharp teeth. "I can see why!"

Blossom took refuge up the cherry blossom tree. The

gate creaked open. It was Lydia. Mandy and James jumped to their feet. "Hi," said Mandy, running over.

"So, where are these kittens, then?" Lydia said, looking around uncertainly.

"Over here," said Mandy, taking Lydia over to the tree. She held her breath as Lydia looked down at the bundles of white, ginger, and tabby fluff. "The white ones are Delilah's, they've all got homes."

Peaches came stalking over and pounced on Lydia's foot with her claws out. Lydia laughed and picked her up. Peaches meowed loudly.

"Well?" said Mandy.

There was a long pause. Lydia looked down at the little kitten in her arms. Peaches blinked up at her, her head on one side. Closing her eyes, she rubbed her face against Lydia's chest. Lydia looked at Mandy and James and her face broke into a smile. "Maybe I do need a cat," she said.

Mandy threw her arms around her, being careful not to crush Peaches at the same time. "Oh, Lydia! That's wonderful!"

"Which one?" James said eagerly.

Lydia looked down at Peaches in her arms. "Do you think this one could catch a few mice?"

"Definitely!" Mandy enthused. "She's great at pouncing. I think she'll be great at hunting when she gets older."

"Then I'll have her." Lydia looked over the other kittens. "He looks like a character," she said, pointing to William, who was halfway down the yard, lying on his back and wrestling with a daffodil.

James grinned. "He certainly is."

"Then I'll have him, too," decided Lydia. "They can keep each other company."

James scooped up little Cherry. "That only leaves Cherry," he said. "She'll be all by herself."

But Lydia wasn't to be swayed. She shook her head firmly. "Two's enough for me."

Mandy sighed. Her plan of having all three in one home didn't look like it was going to work out. Still, at least Peaches and William would be together, and she would be able to see them whenever she went up to High Cross Farm. That was something. She picked William up and brought him over. "He's quite bossy," she said. "He likes having his own way."

Lydia laughed. "Just like the goats." She took William off Mandy. "I can see you and I will get along just fine," she said to the little ginger kitten. She looked down at the two kittens in her arms. "Cats," she said in surprise. "I'm going to have two cats!"

*   *   *

When Mandy got back to Animal Ark that afternoon, she went into the residential unit. Delilah was the only patient in and she looked very bored. Mandy opened the cage and took her out. "You'll be going home soon," she said, cuddling the white cat. She knew it was hard for any animal to have to stay in a cage and rest; cats in particular really hated being confined. She decided to groom her and, finding a brush, sat down on the floor.

Dr. Emily looked around the door. "I thought I heard you come in," she said. She looked at the cat. "How's Delilah today?"

"Bored," said Mandy.

Dr. Emily came over and tickled Delilah's ears. "Bill and Jane are coming to visit her tomorrow, so hopefully that will cheer her up. Anyway, how did it go with Lydia today? Has she decided to have one of the kittens?"

"She's taking two," grinned Mandy. "She loved them. She chose Peaches and William. So it's just Cherry and Blossom who need homes now."

Dr. Emily frowned. "Maybe you should call up Betty Hilder at the Animal Sanctuary. Warn her that you may be bringing them in. It will give her a chance to start looking for homes for them."

"But the Wards don't mind having them in their shed," said Mandy quickly. "If Blossom and Cherry go up to the Sanctuary they will have to go into a cage."

"The cages at the sanctuary are quite roomy. It will be easier for Betty to find a home for Cherry while she's still a little kitten."

"It won't be easy to find a home for Blossom," Mandy argued. "No one wants adult cats. Blossom may be in there for ages. She'll hate it!"

Dr. Emily sighed. "It *is* more difficult to find homes for adult cats," she admitted. "Still, you can't expect the Wards to let Blossom stay in their shed forever. The sooner Betty knows, the better."

"But, Mom . . ."

"No buts, Mandy." Dr. Emily's eyes were firm. "Give Betty a call tomorrow. It's the only sensible thing to do."

Nine

Mandy sat at the kitchen table at Animal Ark and tried to make a list of all the people who might give Blossom a home. It wasn't going very well — in fact, it didn't have any names on it at all. She sighed and chewed the end of her pen. There had to be *someone* she knew who wanted a cat.

Blossom deserved a loving home. She had so many endearing habits: the way she would roll in the flowers; the way she would sit up on her back legs and beg for food and attention; the way she would rub her head against your hand, purring loudly. It was hard to imagine that anyone could have abandoned her.

Dr. Emily came into the kitchen. She was carrying Delilah. "Jane and Bill are coming around," she said. "I thought I'd bring Delilah into the living room. It will be more comfy for them in there. Dad's been called out to a calving." She put Delilah down. "Have you called Betty yet?"

Mandy shook her head.

"Mandy . . ."

"I will, Mom!"

Just then the phone rang. "I'll get it," Mandy exclaimed, seizing the chance to escape. "Hello?" she said quickly.

"Good morning, this is Lydia Fawcett speaking." Lydia had only recently had a telephone connected to High Cross Farm and always sounded rather formal on the phone.

Mandy smiled. "Hi, Lydia. Do you want to speak to Mom?"

"Actually, no. I was calling about the two kittens." Lydia cleared her throat. "I happened to be in town yesterday and while I was there I bought two baskets, some toys, and two bowls. I was wondering if there is any other equipment you would suggest I purchase?"

"I don't think so," said Mandy, rather taken aback. "You sound like you've got everything."

"If I take on a responsibility to an animal, I like to see

it through," said Lydia stiffly. "All the animals at High Cross Farm are looked after to the best of my capabilities."

Mandy smiled. She knew Lydia well enough to realize that underneath the stiff and formal exterior, Lydia was secretly rather excited at the prospect of having the two kittens coming to live at High Cross Farm. William and Peaches really couldn't be going to a better home. "I'm so glad you're having the kittens, Lydia," she said. "They'll be so happy with you."

There was a pause. When Lydia spoke again, her tone had softened slightly. "I am rather looking forward to having them," she admitted.

As Mandy put down the phone, she heard her mother letting the Wards in. Mandy hurried to the living room to see Delilah's reaction. As always when Delilah saw them, her bored expression vanished. She rubbed against their legs, purring nonstop. "Oh, Delilah," said Jane Ward, kneeling on the floor beside her. "You are glad to see us, aren't you?"

Bill rubbed her ears. "There's a good girl. We've been missing you." Delilah's purrs got even louder as she rubbed her head against his face.

"She's getting much better," Dr. Emily said. "We're very pleased with her. If it wasn't for the kittens, I would let her come home with you now. However, it is better to be safe than sorry. Her bones are still at a delicate stage in the healing process. Even though it means her being bored here, I think she should stay until the kittens have gone to their new homes."

"We've decided that we're going to keep Daisy," said Jane. "Will Delilah be all right, when she does come back, if Daisy wants to play?"

"I'll want you to keep a careful eye on the pair of them at first," said Dr. Emily. "But it should be fine."

Jane frowned. "Actually, I've been meaning to ask you a question about Daisy. We've heard you can have cats microchipped so they can be traced if they are lost or stolen. What do you think about it?"

"Good idea," agreed Dr. Emily. "Have you had Delilah done?" Mrs. Ward shook her head. "Well, then I'd recommend that they were both microchipped."

"How dangerous is it?" asked Bill cautiously.

"Not at all," said Dr. Emily. "All it involves is inserting a tiny microchip in the back of the cat's neck, and it means that if they ever get lost and are picked up by a big animal shelter or taken into a police station, then you can be contacted. The microchip is tiny, only about the size of a grain of rice, and yet when it's scanned into a computer it reveals the owner's details. I think all pets should be done. It would prevent an awful lot of heartache."

Mandy stared at her mother as a sudden thought struck her. "Mom! What about Blossom? We've never checked to see if she has a microchip."

Dr. Emily frowned. "No, we haven't." She shrugged. "I guess it might be worth a try."

"Can we go and get her now and see?" asked Mandy. If Blossom did have a microchip, then her owner could be traced and the little cat wouldn't have to adjust to a new home.

Dr. Emily looked at the Wards. "Don't worry about us," said Bill cheerfully. "We'll wait here and spend some time with Delilah, if that's all right with you."

Dr. Emily nodded. "Of course. We won't be long."

Mandy picked up a plastic cat carrier from the office and jumped into the car. "Now don't build your hopes up," Dr. Emily warned. "Not that many cat owners have their cats microchipped."

But Mandy didn't want to listen to her mother's practical warning. "Can I call up James on the cell phone?" she asked. She knew James would be as excited as she was.

Dr. Emily smiled and nodded. James arranged to meet them at Animal Ark so that he could be there when Dr. Emily tested for the microchip. They collected Blossom with no trouble at all, shutting the kittens in the shed so they would be safe until Blossom was returned.

James was waiting at the bottom of the Animal Ark driveway. He cycled up after them. "You really think she might have a microchip?" he asked Mandy as she jumped out of the car.

Mandy nodded. "Fingers crossed!"

The Wards joined them in the consulting room to see if Blossom had had a microchip implanted. They stood to one side with James while Mandy held Blossom firmly on the table. Dr. Emily took a piece of equipment out of a drawer. It looked just like a bar-code scanner at a supermarket checkout. Dr. Emily ran it over Blos-

som's back and neck. "If she has a microchip, then we will hear a bleep," she explained.

There was no sound. "Try again," urged Mandy. She knew that sometimes the chip could move slightly. She crossed her fingers tightly. For one awful moment she thought her hopes were going to have been in vain and then, *bleep*!

Mandy jumped in the air with excitement. "She's got one!" she cried, grabbing James and hugging him. "There it is!" James blushed and she hastily let go of him. "Mom! We can find Blossom's owners!"

Dr. Emily kissed her. "You were right, dear. Well done." She noted down the microchip number the scanner had picked up. "Each microchip has a different number," she said, turning to the Wards. "Now all we need to do is call up the database holders with this number and they should be able to find out Blossom's owner's contact details."

Mandy hugged Blossom impatiently as her mother telephoned the helpline. Dr. Emily reported Animal Ark's authorization code and then the number on Blossom's chip.

"What happens now?" Mandy asked as her mother put down the phone.

"Now they contact the owner," said Dr. Emily.

"And then the owner will contact Animal Ark?" asked James.

Dr. Emily nodded. "But only if the details on the database are still correct — sometimes people forget to update them if they move to another house or if circumstances change." She looked carefully at Mandy and James. "Now I don't want you getting your hopes up. Even if the details are correct and they do reach Blossom's owner, then it is just possible that they might not actually want her back."

Mandy stared. "What do you mean? Of course they'll want her."

Dr. Emily shook her head. "We don't know that for sure. They might have abandoned her on purpose."

Mandy looked down at the little tabby cat in her arms. It was hard to believe that anyone would do such a thing, but then she knew that not everyone felt the way she did about animals. She kissed Blossom's head and then met James's gaze. There was nothing they could do now but wait.

Monday and Tuesday passed slowly. There was no word from Blossom's owners. By Tuesday evening a seed of doubt started to grow in Mandy's mind. Maybe her mom was right. Maybe Blossom's owners didn't want her anymore. The wonderful hopeful feelings began to slowly fizzle away. *It's beginning to look as if we're going to have to find a home for Blossom after all*, she thought, getting out her bike on Wednesday morning.

She called good-bye to her dad, who was just going into the clinic, adjusted her backpack, and set off down the driveway.

"Mandy!" She braked and turned. Dr. Adam was waving from the clinic door.

"What?" she called.

"There's a message on the answering machine I think you might want to hear. It's from Blossom's owner!"

Dropping her bike on the gravel, Mandy raced up to the clinic. She pressed the play button eagerly. "One message. Wednesday, seven fifty-seven A.M.," said the computerized voice. Dr. Adam came up behind her. Mandy glanced at him with excited eyes.

"Umm, hello," came a female voice. "My name is Mrs. Stanley. I've just had a message that you have found my cat. I can come and collect her today about five o'clock. I hope that's okay." There was a pause. "I'd almost given up hope," the voice continued. Mandy had the impression that the woman leaving the message was suddenly fighting back tears. "I've been looking for her for four months, you see. We moved and . . . well, I can tell you when I see you. Bye."

Mandy stared at the answering machine, caught between elation and dismay. Mrs. Stanley sounded like she loved Blossom very much, but now she wanted to come and take her away that day! "What about the kittens!" Mandy exclaimed, turning to her father. "Delilah's kittens are too young to manage without Blossom. They're not weaned yet. She can't take Blossom away tonight!"

"I'm afraid she can, Mandy," Dr. Adam said. "She is Blossom's owner, after all."

Mandy started to shake her head. "No!"

Dr. Adam squeezed her arm. "Come on. Mrs. Stanley may be perfectly reasonable about it and agree to let Blossom stay for a bit longer."

"She should have left a number!" said Mandy. "She's going to arrive and not know about Blossom's kittens. She might not want them." Her eyes widened as an even worse thought crossed her mind. "Or she might want to keep them *all* and then what will Lydia do?" She stared at her father in dismay.

"It's not going to do any good worrying about it," Dr. Adam said reasonably. "Go on, off to school. Everything will work out. You'll see."

But what if it doesn't? thought Mandy as she got back onto her bike. *What if Mrs. Stanley insists on taking Blossom, Cherry, Peaches, and William away?* A lump formed in her throat.

"Hi!" called James as she cycled up. As soon as he saw her face, he frowned. "What's up?"

Mandy had to fight back the tears as she explained. James stared at her in horror. "She can't take away Blossom. Whatever would the Wards do?"

"Someone would have to look after the kittens," Mandy said. "But you know how difficult it is and, anyway, they're at such an important stage in their development. They need a mother." She looked at him desperately. "James, we can't let this happen."

"But what can we do?"

Mandy shook her head. She was thrilled that Blossom wouldn't have to go to the Animal Sanctuary, but she couldn't shake off a feeling of impending doom. "We'll think of something," she said determinedly.

But, for once, Mandy was at a complete loss for ideas. Her dad was right. Mrs. Stanley had every right to take Blossom and her kittens away if she wanted to. As five o'clock drew near, Mandy and James waited uneasily in the reception at Animal Ark. Jean tapped at the computer, smiling at them whenever she looked up.

Mandy tidied up the leaflets and nervously straightened the pile of magazines. James watched out of the window. Dr. Emily was in the treatment room with a beagle puppy and his owner, but she popped her head out. "Any sign of Mrs. Stanley?"

James shook his head. Mandy walked up and down the waiting room.

"There's a car coming," James said, a few minutes later. "Do you recognize it?" Mandy rushed to the window and shook her head. They watched as the woman got out. She was about Dr. Emily's age and was wearing a long navy dress. James raised his eyebrows. "What do you think, Mandy? She doesn't exactly look like a heartless monster."

"But what if she is?" Mandy said nervously.

The door opened and the woman came in.

"Umm, hello," she said, running a hand rather nervously through her short dark hair. She looked from Mandy to James and then at Jean. She was obviously unsure who to talk to. "I've come for my cat. She's here, I believe. My name's Janice Stanley."

Mandy took a deep breath and introduced herself. "My parents are the vets here," she explained. "Your cat isn't here, she's staying at a house nearby. James and I have been helping to look after her."

"But you do have her and she is all right?"

Mandy nodded and saw the relief light up in Mrs. Stanley's eyes. "Actually." Mandy cast a look in James's direction for moral support. "She had kittens." She watched carefully for Mrs. Stanley's reaction.

"Kittens!" she gasped. Mandy and James nodded. "Goodness, I don't know what to say." She rubbed her forehead.

Just then Dr. Emily came out with the beagle and its owner. She realized right away who Mrs. Stanley was, and came over and introduced herself.

"I've just been told about the kittens," Mrs. Stanley said, still sounding rather shocked.

"*All* the kittens?" Dr. Emily asked with a look at Mandy. Mandy shook her head. Mrs. Stanley looked at them in some alarm.

Dr. Emily hastily explained. "Your cat's been a foster mother for four Persian kittens as well as her own three kittens, Mrs. Stanley. The Persians' mother was in a car accident and is recovering here in our residential unit. Before the accident, your cat was living in the owner's yard shed. After the accident she took it upon herself to foster the kittens."

"Oh," said Mrs. Stanley faintly.

The words burst from Mandy. "But they're only five weeks old and still really need her. Please don't take her away just yet! Please let her stay another two weeks!"

Mrs. Stanley looked as if she didn't know what to say.

Dr. Emily smiled at her. "I know this must all come as

a bit of a surprise," she said. "And I'm sure at the moment you just want to see your cat. Why don't you follow me in your car? It's not far." Mrs. Stanley nodded gratefully.

In the car, James looked at Mandy. "Well, what do you think?"

"I don't know," said Mandy with a frown. "She seemed all right but she didn't say much when I asked her whether Blossom could stay."

Dr. Emily shook her head as she started the engine. "You hardly gave the poor woman a chance, Mandy. She was completely taken aback and I hardly blame her. Her cat's been missing for four months. She turns up to collect her, only to be told that she's had kittens, she's fostering another litter, and that you don't want her taken away just yet."

Mandy felt her face go a bit pink. "I guess so."

They arrived at the Wards to find Bill and Jane waiting anxiously in the garden. Dr. Emily had phoned them earlier in the day to tell them the news. Mandy and James ran to meet them.

"What's she like?" Mrs. Ward asked Mandy. "Do you think she will let Blossom stay?"

Before Mandy could reply, Mrs. Stanley arrived. She came through the gate and crossed the grass eagerly toward them. She suddenly stopped dead. "Blossom," she whispered, staring at the tabby cat sitting in a patch of late afternoon sunlight. "Blossom, is it really you?"

"How did you know that was what we called her?" Mandy asked.

James nudged her to be quiet and nodded toward Blossom. The little cat had stiffened at the sound of her owner's voice. Her tabby ears pricked and the next minute she was bounding over the grass, heading straight as an arrow for Mrs. Stanley.

Mrs. Stanley bent down and opened her arms. The little cat put her paws up on Mrs. Stanley's shoulders and started rubbing her head frantically against her cheek.

"Oh, Blossom!" cried Mrs. Stanley. "I'm so glad to see you."

As she straightened up, Mandy repeated the question that was burning on her lips. "But how did you know we called her Blossom?"

"I didn't," said Mrs. Stanley. "That's her name. You mean, you called her Blossom, too?"

Mandy explained how the name had come about.

"But that's just why I called her Blossom in the first place," said Mrs. Stanley, in astonishment. "I saw her rolling in the blossoms when she was a tiny kitten."

Mandy grinned. "No wonder she seemed to learn it so quickly!"

"I think it's time for some human introductions," said Dr. Emily. She introduced the Wards.

"It's our cat, Delilah, who was in the accident," Jane explained. "Blossom's been helping us out by looking after the kittens."

"Jane and Bill started feeding Blossom when she first came into the yard," said Dr. Emily.

"Well, we noticed she was a bit thin," said Bill. "And expecting kittens, too."

Mandy noticed Mrs. Stanley smiling gratefully. "Mr. and Mrs. Ward have really been wonderful," Mandy said. "They gave Blossom a home and made friends with her, and helped when she was ill having her kittens." She glanced at James and he took the hint.

"They even cleared out all the things from their shed and put them into their spare room so that Blossom and the kittens would be safe," he said.

"You've all been so kind," said Mrs. Stanley, looking around. "I really can't thank you enough."

"The kittens will be completely weaned in another couple of weeks," said Mandy, her eyes pleading with Mrs. Stanley. "If Blossom could just stay until then?"

Mrs. Stanley's eyes were torn. "I know they need Blossom, it's just . . ." She looked down at Blossom in her arms. "I've missed her so much. We were moving from Walton when she disappeared. I searched every-where, came back every day, but there was no sign of her. I was starting to give up hope when I got the mes-sage. I know I should leave her here, I know it's the right thing to do" — her voice choked up a bit — "but I just don't know if I can bear to do it."

Mandy glanced anxiously at James. Somehow they had to make Mrs. Stanley see how important it was that Blossom stay.

"Look out! One of the kittens has found a bee!" Dr. Emily exclaimed.

Everyone looked around, alarmed. Over by the tree, a large bumblebee was crawling slowly across the grass. Daisy was staring at it, fascinated. She patted at it with her paw. The bee buzzed angrily. Daisy put her head to one side. "She's going to try to eat it!" exclaimed Mandy, recognizing the expression on Daisy's face.

"Someone stop her!" gasped Mrs. Stanley.

Before anyone could move, Blossom had twisted out of Mrs. Stanley's arms, streaked across the grass, and reached the little kitten. With one swipe of her paw, she knocked Daisy firmly out of harm's way. Daisy rolled over on her back. The bumbleebee crawled safely away.

Everyone sighed with relief. "That was lucky," said Dr. Emily. "If Daisy had swallowed the bee, there's a chance it would have stung her and the swelling might have blocked up her throat."

Mandy raced over and scooped up Daisy. "Oh, Daisy, you silly kitten, that was very dangerous," she said. "You mustn't play with bees." She brought her back to where the others were standing.

"The bee must have been waking up after the winter. That's why it was going so slowly," said Dr. Emily.

"At least Daisy's all right," said Mandy, cuddling the little kitten.

"Can I hold her?" asked Mrs. Stanley, rather shyly. Mandy handed Daisy to her. Mrs. Stanley looked down at the kitten in her arms. "I guess I can't take Blossom away, can I?" she said. "They really do need her."

Mandy felt her heart leap. "It's only for another two weeks, Mrs. Stanley."

"And you can come and visit," said Jane Ward, her face lighting up with delight. "Anytime you want."

"It really will make a tremendous difference, Mrs. Stanley," Dr. Emily put in warmly.

Mrs. Stanley cheered up. "At least at the end of it, I'll have Blossom and three kittens to take home. That's certainly something to look forward to."

"What will you do with the kittens?" asked James. "Will you keep them all?"

Mandy held her breath and waited for the answer.

"I'd love to, but I really haven't the room. I'll keep just one." Mrs. Stanley looked to where little Cherry was rolling in the flowers on the grass. "And I don't think I'll have to think too hard about which one it will be."

"Cherry?" said Mandy, following her gaze.

"She looks just like Blossom did at that age." Mrs. Stanley smiled. "Don't worry, though, I'll make sure I find good homes for the other two."

"But we've already found them a wonderful home!" The words burst out of Mandy. "A home together on a farm."

Mrs. Stanley looked rather surprised. "Oh."

"It was all arranged before Mandy had the idea of looking to see whether Blossom had a microchip," said Dr. Emily quickly. "It really would be an excellent home for them, Mrs. Stanley, if you don't have any definite plans."

Mandy waited anxiously. Mrs. Stanley smiled. "Well, in that case, I'm certainly not going to argue. After all, the most important thing is that all the kittens are happy."

Smiling broadly, Jane invited everyone in for a cup of tea. As the adults set off to the house, James nudged Mandy. "So, Mrs. Stanley's a monster, then?" he said slyly.

Mandy grinned and, in reply, picked up a handful of blossoms and stuck them down his back.

Dr. Emily drove the Land Rover slowly back through the village. "I can't believe it's worked out so well," said Mandy contentedly. "We don't have to say good-bye to Blossom just yet, after all."

"Delilah's kittens will have her as a mom for a bit longer," said James.

"Peaches and William are going to go and live at High Cross Farm," said Mandy.

"And Delilah is well on the way to making a full recovery," put in Dr. Emily.

Mandy looked happily at James. "Isn't life great?"